Henry Inman

Tales of the Trail

Short Stories of Western Life

Henry Inman

Tales of the Trail
Short Stories of Western Life

ISBN/EAN: 9783744649919

Printed in Europe, USA, Canada, Australia, Japan

Cover: Foto ©Andreas Hilbeck / pixelio.de

More available books at **www.hansebooks.com**

TALES OF THE TRAIL

SHORT STORIES OF WESTERN LIFE

BY

COLONEL HENRY INMAN

Late Assistant Quartermaster, United States Army

AUTHOR OF "THE OLD SANTA FÉ TRAIL," "SALT LAKE TRAIL"

CRANE & COMPANY, PUBLISHERS

TOPEKA, KANSAS

1898

PREFACE.

THESE "Tales of the Trail" are based upon
actual facts which came under the personal observation of the author, whose reputation as a
writer of the frontier is national. His other
works have met with phenomenal success, and
these sketches, which have appeared from time
to time in the current literature of the United
States, are now compiled, and will form another
interesting series of stories of that era of great
adventures, when the country west of the Missouri was unknown except to the trappers,
hunters, and army officers.

Some of the characters around which are
woven the thrilling incidents of these "Tales"
were men of world-wide reputation; they have
long since joined the "choir invisible," but their
names as pioneers in the genesis of great States
which then formed the theater of their exploits
will live as long as the United States exists as
a great nation.

However improbable to the uninitiated the
thrilling experiences of the individuals who

were actors in the scenes depicted, may seem, they are a proof that "truth is stranger than fiction."

It is fortunate that Colonel Inman during his forty years on the extreme frontier was such a close observer, and noted from time to time these stories of the frontier which form such an interesting part of our Americana.

JAMES L. KING,
State Librarian.

TOPEKA, KANSAS, March 1, 1898.

CONTENTS.

ILLUSTRATIONS.

GEN. FORSYTHE AT THE ARRICKAREE.

A THRILLING STORY OF INDIAN WARFARE.

GENERAL FORSYTHE.

I WAS sitting in my office at Fort Harker on a warm evening in the latter part of September, 1868, musing over a pipeful of "Lone Jack," upon the possible extent of the impending Indian war, which had already been planned by Gen. Sheridan, in the seclusion of my own quarters, only the night before. It was rapidly growing dark; the somber line of the twilight curve had almost met the western horizon, and only the faintest tinge of purple beneath marked the intermedium between the gloaming and the rayless sky.

Nothing disturbed my revery as I wandered in my imagination over the bleak expanse of the Arkansas, Cimarron and Canadian rivers, so soon to be the scene of active operations, except the monotonous clicking of the relay in the window of the next room, where the Government night operator was on duty, who was also meditating in the darkness.

The terrible massacres on Spillman creek, only a few weeks before, still furnished food for vengeful thoughts that would not down, as images of the murdered women and little ones rose in horrible visions upon the thick night before me.

The dismal howl of a hungry wolf borne upon the still air from the timbered recesses of the Smoky added to the weird aspect that my surroundings were rapidly assuming, and there seemed some portentous and indescribable thing bearing down upon the place.

Suddenly the operator—while the clicking of the instruments became more nervous and varied from their monotone of the whole evening—exclaimed, "My God! Major, what's this?"

"What is what?" said I, jumping from my chair and rushing to his side. Quickly lighting his little lamp and seizing his pencil, he wrote upon a blank as I looked over his shoulder and read—while the clicking grew more convulsive still—these words:

"Gen. Forsythe surrounded by Indians on the Republican. Lieut. Beecher, the doctor, and many of the scouts killed; nearly the entire command, including the general, wounded. Stillwell, one of the scouts, ran the gauntlet of the savages, and brings report. Col. Carpenter, Tenth Cavalry, and his command, leave immediately to relieve them."

This was a fragment of the whole dispatch going over the wires from Fort Hays to Fort Leavenworth and Washington. We had taken enough of it to know that a terrible disaster had befallen the gallant Forsythe, of Sheridan's staff, and his plucky band of scouts, who were all civilians and Kansans.

The headquarters of Gen. Sheridan, who was at the date of this narrative in command of the Department of the Missouri, were temporarily established at Fort Harker. He was consummating his arrangements for a winter campaign against the hostile tribes, and the idea suggested itself that a body of carefully selected men, composed of the best material to be found on the frontier, under the leadership of an experienced officer, could effect excellent results.

These scouts, as they were to be termed, were to go anywhere, and act entirely independent of the regularly organized troops about to take the field.

Generals Custer and Sully, the next in rank to Sheridan, both already famous as Indian fighters, coincided with this view of the commanding general; and it was determined to pick fifty equipped frontiersmen at once, commission Forsythe as their leader, who in the incipiency of the movement modestly solicited the responsible position.

The fifty-four men were chosen from an aggregate of more than 2,000 employed by the Government at various positions at Forts Harker and Hays. The reader may rest assured that only those were accepted who possessed the essential qualifications of indomitable courage, wonderful endurance, perfect markmanship, and a thorough knowledge of the Indian character.

Gen. Forsythe chose for his lieutenant his particular friend F. H. Beecher, of the Third Infantry, a nephew of the celebrated Brooklyn clergyman.

Some days were occupied at Fort Harker in fitting out the little expedition, but no unneces-

sary equipage or superfluous camp paraphernalia
formed any part of the supplies.

There were no tents or wagons. Pack-mules
carried the commissary stores, which were of the
simplest character, and as the object of the party
was war, its impedimenta were reduced to the
minimum.

Each man was mounted on an excellent horse,
his armament a breech-loading rifle and two revolvers.

This troop of brave men left Harker for Hays
in the latter part of August, from which point
their arduous duties were commenced.

On the 29th of that month, all the preliminaries for taking the field having been completed
and their surgeon joined, they marched out of the
fort on their perilous mission. After scouting
over a large area for several days without meeting
any sign of the Cheyennes, they concluded to go to
Wallace to recuperate and refit.

Sometime during the second week in September
the Indians made a raid on a Government wagon
train near Sheridan station, on the Kansas Pacific
Railroad, about twelve miles east of Wallace. As
soon as the news reached the fort over the wires,
Forsythe and his little band of scouts started to
intercept the savages on their retreat.

Next morning the little command struck the'
fresh trail of the Indians, and by forced marches
came so close that they compelled them to separate into insignificant detachments, but night
coming rapidly on, the General lost the trail.
The conclusion was, after a consultation with the
best plainsmen among the party, that the Indians
would naturally go northward; so it was determined to take that direction in pursuit.

The scouts continued their course for more
than a week without the least trifling incident
to relieve the wearisome monotony of the march.

Suddenly, on the afternoon of the eighth day,
as they were approaching the bluffs of the Republican river, they discovered an immense trail
still leading to the north. The signs indicated
that a large body of warriors, with pack animals,
women and children, and lodges of a big camp,
had recently camped there.

It was growing dark, and rather than take the
chances of losing this trail in the night, it was
determined to bivouac in the vicinity, rest the
animals, and continue the pursuit at the first
streak of dawn.

It was well that this course was decided upon,
or there would have been none left to tell the
story of the fight, as the result will show. The

spot selected for the bivouac had some slight
strategic value, and was for that reason chosen
by the General, after it had been pointed out by
two of his men, Tom Murphy and Jack Stillwell;
though he had no idea at the time that any
benefit would result from their judgment in this
particular. It was an elongated low mound of
sand (such as are seen at intervals in the Arkansas) which the Arrickaree fork of the Republican at this time embraced (as the Cheyenne
does the Black Hills), forming an island.

If this trail had not been struck, it was the
intention to have gone back to Wallace for provisions, as only sufficient for one day remained;
but upon prospects of a fight, it was unanimously
agreed to go, and take the chances of finding
something to eat.

In the early gray of the next morning, while
the stars were still twinkling and at the hour
when sleep oppresses more than at any other
time, the sentinels posted on the hills above the
island yelled, "Indians!"

In a moment the camp was awake. With rifle
in hand, each scout rushed for the lariat to
which his horse was picketed, knowing of course
that the first effort on the part of the Indians
would be to stampede the animals. As it was,

a small party of them dashed in with a horrid whoop, and shaking their buffalo robes, succeeded in running off a small portion of the pack-mules, besides one or two of the horses.

A few shots fired by the most advanced of the scouts scattered the Indians, and quiet reigned again for a few minutes.

Almost immediately, however, before the scouts had completed saddling their horses—which the General had ordered—one of the guides nearest Forsythe happening to look up, could not help giving vent to the expression, "Great heavens! General, see the Indians!"

Well might he be excited. Over the hills, from the west and north, along the river on the opposite bank—everywhere, and in every direction, they made their appearance. Finely mounted, in full war paint, their long scalp-locks braided with eagles' feathers, and with all the paraphernalia of a barbarous war party, with wild and exultant shouts, on they came.

It was a desperate-looking preponderance of brute force and savage subtlety, against the cool and calm judgment of the disciplined plainsmen. But the General, without glancing at the hell in front and all around him, with only the lines of determination in his face a little more marked,

grasping the terrible picture before him, stoically
ordered his men to take possession of the sand
mound with their horses, and then determined,
almost against hope, to accept the wager of
battle.

It happened, fortunately, that on this island
were growing some stunted shrubs, to which the
animals were fastened, their bodies forming a cor-
don, inside of which the luckless scouts prepared
for the demoniacal charge which they knew must
come with its terrible uncertainty in a few minutes.

They had scarcely secured their animals, when
like the shock of a whirlwind on came the savages, and the awfully unequal battle commenced.

It was just the break of dawn; the Indians,
taking advantage of the uncertain light, dismounted from their ponies, and creeping within
easy range, poured in a murderous fire upon the
scouts.

The Indians were splendidly armed as usual,
through the munificence of the Government, by
its apathy in preventing renegade white men or
traders from supplying them.

When the full morning came, which had been
anxiously waited for by the scouts, then they
first realized their desperate situation. Appar-

ently as numerous as the sand-grains of their little fortification, the Indians hemmed them in on all sides. More than a thousand hideously painted and screaming warriors surrounded them, with all their hatred of the race depicted on their fiendish countenances, in anticipation of the victory which seemed so certain.

Scattered among these, out of rifle-range, were the squaws and children of the aggregated band, watching with gloating eyes the progress of the battle, while the hills reëchoed their diabolical death-chant and the howling of the medicine-men inspiring the young warriors to deeds of daring.

No one can form the slightest conception of the horrid picture spread before the scouts on the clear gray of that morning, unless he or she has realized it in the hostile encounters with the hostile tribes on the plains. Language is inadequate, and all the attempts at word-painting fall so short of the reality that it were better left wrapped in its terrible incomprehensibleness.

The General and his brave men took in their chances at a glance. They saw little hope in the prospect, but they determined, however, never to be taken alive—a thousand deaths by the bullet were preferable to that; so made up their minds to fight to the bitter end, which would only come when the ammunition was exhausted or themselves killed.

To this end they commenced to intrench as best they could, by scraping holes in the sand with the only implement at their command—their hands. They succeeded in making a sort of rifle-pit of their position, but before the work was completed, two of the scouts were killed outright, and many wounded—among the latter the General himself.

Owing to the dreadful firing of the Indians, who continually charged down upon the island, the doctor was compelled to abandon the care of the wounded and become a combatant; he did excellent work with his rifle, but a bullet soon pierced his brain, and he too fell dead.

In a few seconds after the doctor's death, in the midst of a terrible onslaught by the Indians, the General was again struck—this time near the ankle, the ball perforating the bone as perfectly as if done with an auger.

The firing of the scouts had not all this time been without telling effect upon the Indians—many a painted warrior had bitten the dust before the sun was two hours high. At each successive charge of the redskins, the scouts, cool and careful, and deliberate, took aim, and when their rifles were discharged each put a savage *hors de combat*—there was no ammunition wasted!

Nor had the besieged escaped from the fearful onset of their enemies: besides the casualties related, nearly all the horses had been killed—in fact, before noon all but one had fallen, and it is. told that when he too was killed, one of the warriors exclaimed in English, "There goes the last horse, anyway!"

At this juncture, with all their horses killed or wounded, the Indians determined upon one more grand charge which would settle the unequal contest. So they rallied all their forces and hazarded their reputation upon the aggregated assault.

This charging column was composed of about one hundred and fifty "dog soldiers" and nearly five hundred more of the Brulés, Cheyennes, and Arapahoes, all under the command of the celebrated chief "Roman Nose."

Superbly mounted, almost naked, although in full war dress, and painted in the most hideous manner, formed with a front of about sixty men, they awaited in the greatest confidence the signal of their chief to charge.

Their leader at first signaled to the dismounted men beyond this line of horsemen to fire into the scouts, and thus make his contemplated charge more effective. At the moment of the fusillade, seeing the little garrison was stunned by the fire of the dismounted Indians, and rightly judging that now if ever was the proper time to charge, Roman Nose and his band of mounted warriors,

THE CHARGE.

with a wild ringing war-whoop, echoed by the women and children on the hills, started forward.

On they came, presenting even to the brave men awaiting their charge, a most superb sight.

Soon they were within the range of the rifles of their friends, and of course the dismounted Indians had to slacken their fire for fear of hitting their own warriors.

And this was the opportunity for the scouts.

"Now!" shouted Forsythe; and the scouts, springing to their knees, cast their eyes coolly along the
barrels of their rifles, and opened upon the ad-
vancing savages a deadly fire.

Unchecked, undaunted, on dashed the warriors.
Steadily rang the sharp report of the rifles of the
frontiersmen. Roman Nose falls dead from his
horse; "Medicine Man" is killed; and for an instant the column, now within ten feet of the
scouts, hesitates — falters.

A cheer from the scouts, who perceive the effect
of their well-directed fire, as the Indians begin to
break and scatter in every direction, unwilling to
rush into a hand-to-hand struggle. A few more
shots, and the Indians are forced back beyond
range.

Forsythe inquires anxiously, "Can they do better than that, Grover?"

"I have been on the plains, General, since a
boy, and never saw such a charge as that before."

"All right, then; we are good for them."

It was in this grand charge, led in person by
their greatest of all warriors, Roman Nose, that
Lieut. Beecher was mortally wounded. He suffered intensely, and lingered some hours before
his manly spirit was extinguished.

He and I were warmly attached to one another.

I knew full well the generous impulses of his warm young heart, and his perfect unselfishness. He was brave, the very soul of honor, and a favorite in all garrisons.

Before night closed in on the terrible tragedy of that day, the Indians charged on the weary and beleagured scouts again and again, but were as often driven back by the dreadful accuracy of the rifles of the besieged, with an increasing loss each time.

The darkness which had been earnestly looked for at last brought the welcome respite, and it was made possible for the unfortunate men to steal a moment's rest, that was needed, oh, how much!

Hungry, exhausted, with an empty commissariat, every animal dead, their comrades lying stark upon the dreary sand, and a great number writhing in all the agony of torturing wounds; a relentless enemy ever watching; no skilled hand to alleviate the sufferings of the dying, and the only hope of help that might never come, more than a hundred miles away.

Think of that; grasp it if you can!

Later, while the night yet thickened, preparations were made to meet the events that were sure to come with the morning's light, and the little fort—for it had certainly now reached the dignity of that title—was made still stronger. For gabions, the swollen carcasses of the dead horses were used, and huge slices were cut from their thighs for food. Thank God, the torturings of thirst were not added to their other sufferings, for water was easily obtained by digging a short distance.

Thus strengthened, a midnight council of war was held in whisperings, and it was determined to send two of their number to Fort Wallace, as desperate as the undertaking was. A mere boy, Stillwell, and another, Truedell, expressed their willingness to make the attempt.

The brave men crawled from the "island" to run the gauntlet of the watchful savages, ever on the alert to take advantage of the least unfavorable demonstration on the part of their prey, as they fully believed them.

We will leave them making their way cautiously but hopefully in the darkness, for it is not the purpose of the writer at this time to tell of the noble efforts of these brave messengers in their hairbreadth escapes on their lonesome and perilous journey; but let us turn to the worn-out and wounded band of heroes again, to learn how they fared during the long days before help could possibly reach them, even were Stillwell and his companion able to reach Wallace.

The sun rose in all the splendor of a Kansas autumn morning, but the landscape bore the same horrid features of the day before. All through the weary hours the Indians kept up an incessant firing, though no serious charge was attempted — they had had more than they had anticipated, in their efforts in that direction yesterday. The scouts, now pretty effectually intrenched, suffered but little from the wild firing of their besiegers, but it was annoying, and kept the brave men ever prepared for a possible charge, the result of which might not be so fortunate as former ones.

Night again came to throw its mantle of rest upon the little band, and shortly after dark two more scouts were sent out to reach Fort Wallace, if possible; but they failed to get beyond the line of watchful savages, and were compelled to abandon the idea.

This unsuccessful attempt to go for help cast a gloom over the little command, for it could not yet be known what had been the fate of the other two who had gone out the night previously.

The next day the state of affairs assumed a more cheerful aspect — if that could be possible. The squaws and children had disappeared, indi-

—2

cating a retreat upon the part of the Indians, although they still kept up their firing at intervals: perhaps they, too, were getting short of ammunition and provisions.

In the afternoon the savages hoisted a white rag upon a pole and expressed a desire to talk, but our heroes were too wary to be caught with such chaff as that, for with Indians a flag of truce means a massacre, half the time.

That night two more men were sent out, and these carried that famous dispatch of Forsythe's, which should hold its place in history with that other memorable one of Grant's: "I intend to fight it out on this line if it takes all summer." Forsythe's read:

"I am on a little island, and have still plenty of ammunition left. We are living on mule- and horse-meat, and are entirely out of rations. If it were not for so many wounded I would come on and take the chance of whipping them if attacked. They are evidently sick of their bargain. I can hold out six days longer if absolutely necessary; but lose no time."

The morning of the fourth day, on the now historic island, broke somewhat more cheerful still. The Indians could be seen moving rapidly away,

only a few comparatively remaining in sight, to
wait till exhaustion and starvation should place
the scouts in their power. They little knew the
metal of the men lying behind those breastworks
of rotten carcasses, or they too would have gone
with the old men, women and children of the
tribe.

A few shots were fired by the scouts in response
to the occasional random fusillade of the Indians: they contented themselves with saving their
ammunition for a possible last grand act in the
drama, only shooting when an Indian came within
certain range, when he was sure to be sent to the
"happy hunting-grounds."

Night again came with its relative rest, and
then another weary day of watching and waiting,
without any special demonstration on the part of
the Indians.

New horrors now made their appearance in the
shape of gangrened wounds, and suffering for
food. The putrid flesh of the dead horses and
mules was all that remained to support life, and
however revolting, it had to be swallowed. The
nauseating effluvia of the rapidly decaying carcasses, too, made the place almost intolerable,
and so insufferable did it become that the General
told those who were disheartened to go; but all to

a man, to their honor be it recorded, refused, electing to remain with their companions-in-arms —to be rescued, or die with them.

Two more days of torture, and then, on the ridge between them and the golden sunlight gleamed the bright bayonets of Col. Carpenter and his column of "the boys in blue."

Their Havelock had reached this American Lucknow, and cheer after cheer—feeble though they were—went up from the little island, and our story closes with the rescue of these brave men.

GENERAL FORSYTHE (himself wounded in both legs) gives a very graphic description of the charge of the Indians, and the appearance of their hero and chief, Roman Nose. He says:

"As Roman Nose dashed gallantly forward and swept into the open at the head of his superb command, he was the very *beau-ideal* of an Indian chief. Mounted on a large, clean-limbed chestnut horse, he sat well forward on his bareback charger, his knees passing under a horsehair lariat that twice loosely encircled the animal's body, his horse's bridle grasped in his left hand, which was also closely wound in its flowing mane, and at the same time clutched his rifle at the guard, the butt of which lay partially across the animal's neck, while its barrel, crossing diagonally in front of his body, rested slightly against the hollow of his left arm, leaving his right free to direct the course of his men. He was a man over six feet three inches in height, beautifully formed, and save for a crimson silk sash knotted around his waist and his moccasins on his feet, perfectly naked. His face was hideously painted in alternate lines of red and black, and his head crowned with a magnificent war-bonnet, from which, just above his temples and curving slightly forward, stood up two short black buffalo horns, while its ample length of eagles' feathers and herons' plumes trailed wildly on the wind behind him; and as he came swiftly on at the head of his charging warriors, in all his barbaric strength and grandeur, he proudly rode that day the most perfect type of a savage warrior it has been my lot to see. Turning his face for an instant toward the women and children of the united tribes, who literally by thousands were watching the fight from the crest of the low bluffs back from the river's bank, he raised his right arm and waved his right hand with a royal gesture, in answer to their wild cries of rage and encouragement as he and his com-

mand swept down upon us; and again, facing
squarely towards where we lay, he drew his body to
its full height and shook his clenched fist defiantly
at us; then, throwing back his head and glancing
skyward, he suddenly struck the palm of his hand
across his mouth and gave tongue to a war-cry
that I have never yet heard equaled in power and
intensity. Scarcely had its echos reached the
river's bank when it was caught up by each and
every one of the charging warriors with an energy
that baffles description, and answered back with
blood-curdling yells of exultation and prospective
vengeance by the women and children on the
river's bluff and by the Indians who lay in am-
bush around us. On they came at a swinging
gallop, rending the air with their wild war-
whoops, each individual warrior in all his bravery
of war paint and long braided scalp-lock tipped
with eagles' feathers, and all stark naked but for
their cartridge belts and moccasins, keeping their
line almost perfectly, with a front of about sixty
men all riding horseback, with only a loose lariat
about their horses' bodies, and about a yard apart,
and with a depth of six or seven ranks, forming
together a compact body of massive fighting
strength, and of almost resistless weight. 'Boldly
they rode and well,' with their horses' bridles in

their left hands, while with their right they grasped their rifles at the guard and held them squarely in front of themselves, resting lightly upon their horses' necks.

"Riding about five paces in front of the center of the line, and twirling his heavy Springfield rifle about his head as if it were a wisp of straw, Roman Rose recklessly led the charge with a bravery that could only be equaled but not excelled; while their medicine-man, an equally brave yet older chief, rode slightly in advance of the left of the charging column.

"To say that I was surprised at this splendid exhibition of pluck and discipline, is to put it mildly; and to say, further, that for an instant or two I was fairly lost in admiration of the glorious charge, is simply to state the truth — for it was far and away beyond anything I had heard of, read about, or even imagined regarding Indian warfare."

EL SOLITARIO, THE HERMIT PRIEST OF THE OLD SANTA FÉ TRAIL.

"No stream from its source
Flows seaward, how lonely so 'er its course,
But some land is gladden'd. No star ever rose
And set without influence somewhere. Who knows
What earth needs from earth's lowliest creatures?
No life
Can be pure in its purpose, and strong in its strife,
And all life not be purer and stronger thereby."

— OWEN MEREDITH.

T HE tourist *en route* to the Pacific coast cannot fail observing on his right a huge, relatively isolated peak, cutting the incomparably clear mid-continent sky, almost immediately after the train emerges from the picturesque cañon of El Moro, and commences to descend the long gradual slope to

THE HERMIT PRIEST.

24

the quaint old Mexican village of Las Vegas,
New Mexico. Its scarred and verdureless front
looms up grandly in the beautifully serrated
landscape, of which it is the most conspicuous
object. More prominently defined than any
other individual elevation of the Taos Range
visible from the point of observation, the shadow
of its irregular contour reaches far out over the
lesser mountains beneath, the moment the sun
has crossed the meridian of its crest.

At its foot, grassy little valleys stretch east-
wardly, which are cultivated by the primitive
Mexicans under a system of irrigation as primitive as themselves — simple earth ditches, involv-
ing a very limited knowledge of engineering.

Foaming little torrents splash and sparkle in
the sunshine, as they course through the fertile
intervales. Their sources are cool mountain
springs hidden in the dark recesses of the tower-
ing range, which were, until the restless "Gringo"
invaded the solitude of the charming region at
the advent of the iron trail to erect saw-mills,
filled with that most epicurean and gamy of all
the finny tribe, the speckled brook-trout. Now,
the disciple of the revered Walton vainly essays
the streams with elegant modern appliances for
lazy methods of angling, retiring disgusted, as

the listless native, answering his interrogatory of
"Where have they all gone?" with a characteristic shrug, and his ever-ready "Quien sabe?"
quietly opens his little ditch to let the tenantless
water overflow his limited patch of corn, beans,
and onions.

Maybe, in the sad and weird mythology of those
strange people the Aztecs, this storm-beaten spur
of the Rockies occupied an important place.
Their Olympus, or Parnassus perhaps, for not
many miles remote, on the bank of the classic
Pecos, where lie the ruins of the once fortified
Cicuye, referred to so graphically in the itinerary
of the historian of Coronado's wonderful march
in search of the "Seven Cities of Cibola," is the
reputed birthplace of their culture-hero, Monte-
zuma (not to be confounded with the dynasty of
sovereigns of that name), who was the Christ of
their faith, for whose second advent the Pueblos,
the lineal descendants of the Aztecs, look for so
hopefully with the rising of every morning's sun.

Upon the summit of the Rincon de Tecolote,
"The Owl's Corner," now known as "El Cumbre
del Solitario" (The Hermit's Peak), as this grand
old sentinel of the range is called by the Mexicans, an area comprising several acres, there is a
remarkable cave. Around this natural grotto at

such a great elevation, are clustered by the simple natives the most cherished memories of the humble and beloved curious individual who once occupied the sequestered spot. It is sacred ground with them, upon which no sacrilege would for a moment be brooked.

Near its narrow entrance a spring of clear cold water gushes out of the indurated rock, which, after flowing for a short distance over the rounded pebbles in its deeply worn bed, tumbles down the precipitous side of the mountain in a diminutive cascade, joining the streams in the valley on their resistless way to the sea. A few scattered piñons cast a grateful shade over a portion of the generally bald blear level of the limited plain, and at regular distances apart, in the form of a circle, are twelve rude crosses, typical of the number of the Apostles. They were erected years ago by the humble Mexicans living in the hamlets below, in memory of the deeply religious man who made his home in this sequestered spot, and whose name is revered only a degree less than that of the tutelary saint of the country, Our Lady of Guadalupe. On certain feast-days, particularly in midsummer, large fires are kept burning at night, and the devotees to the memory of the cave's once holy occupant, long since hastened by the hand of an assassin to the unknown beyond, assemble there under the stars, and in a most devout spirit perform certain ceremonies, with a zeal possible only to the earnest believers in that ancient and widely disseminated faith, the Catholic religion.

Of the history of this remarkable man, who by his exemplary life made such an impression upon the untutored minds of a large number of the degraded primitive New-Mexicans, but fragmentary leaves have been obtainable. To intelligently understand even these, the reader must let his mind drift backward for more than a generation to the plains of central Kansas, and learn of his advent into the State as I recall it.

It was late in the spring of 1861. Our Civil War had been inaugurated by the firing upon Sumter, and the loyal States were preparing for the great impending struggle, upon the result of which depended the destiny of the Republic. Kansas at that time, so far as its agricultural possibilities were concerned, was not materially considered in that connection; it was a remote, relatively unknown Territory. It is true, its eastern portion, a narrow belt contiguous to Missouri, had a bloody political history; beyond which fact, it was merely the portal to the vast mountain region on the west, to be reached only

by crossing the "Desert" supposed to be in-
cluded within the new State's geographical limits, through which ran the trail to far-off Santa
Fé and Chihuahua.

There arrived one morning in the busy little
hamlet of Council Grove, Morris county, Kansas,
during the month of May, a strange, mysterious.
person. He attracted much attention, for he was
to the denizens of that remote frontier town as
curious a personage as the Man in the Iron Mask,
or the awkward Kaspar Hauser, whose appearance
at the gates of Nuremburg once startled the good
people of that staid and quiet town, hoary with
the conservatism of centuries.

The stranger who came so unexpectedly to
Council Grove in the spring of 1861, evidently a
priest, talked but little; it was an exceedingly
difficult task to engage him in conversation, so
profoundly did he seem impressed with the idea
of some impending danger. He acted like a
startled deer, ever on the alert for an expected
enemy, and weeks rolled by before two or three of
the town's most reputable citizens could gain his
confidence sufficiently to learn from him something of his varied and romantic history. In a
simple sketch, as this is intended to be only,
nothing but a mere outline of his checkered life

previous to his advent in America can be presented, as it was gathered, very reluctantly on his
part, in detached fragments at odd moments in
his erratic moods of communicativeness. It certainly contains enough of pathos, suffering and
tragedy to form the web of a thrilling novel.

Matteo Boccalini, at the date of his appearance
in Council Grove, was about fifty-five years old.
He possessed the eye of an artist, a head that
was beautifully symmetrical, with a classically
moulded face; and notwithstanding his age, his
hair, of which he had a profusion, was long,
black, and lustrous as a raven's wing. Yet the
heart-sorrows he had experienced were indelibly
impressed upon his benevolent countenance in
deeply marked lines. He was a lineal descendant
of Trajano Boccalini, the witty Italian satirist,
author of the celebrated " Ragguagli di Parnaso,"
who died in Venice in 1618. Matteo was born
about the beginning of the present century, in
Capri, that charming and most romantic island
of Italy, situated in the Mediterranean, at the
entrance to the Bay of Naples, twenty miles south
of the beautiful city whose name the bright waters bear.

His youth was passed on the island, in the city
of Capri, the seat of a bishopric. There he re-

ceived his early education, devoting himself to the Church, and commencing those theological studies which were soon to be the cause of his sufferings, his wanderings, and eventually his tragic death.

The island of his birth, which has so often been sung by the muse, is historic as well as picturesquely beautiful. It was there that the Roman emperor Tiberius passed the closing decade of his life, and the ruins of the twelve gorgeous palaces he erected during that period are still visible. Capri, too, as tourists well remember, is famous for a cavern called the "Grotto of the Nymphs," or the "Blue Grotto." Matteo declared it was there that during his youth, in the calm recesses and sequestered nooks of that delightful underground retreat, he first learned to love the companionship of his own thoughts, a desire for solitude, and that to him indescribable peace which a life apart from the "madding crowd" assures. It was this strange characteristic, absence of that love of gregariousness common to man, which earned for him in Council Grove half a century later, the sobriquet of "The Hermit Priest of the Santa Fé Trail," and a year after his departure from that place, among his devoted adherents in the mountains of New Mexico, the more applicable one, "El Solitario" (The Solitary Man), in contradistinction to "El Hermito" (The Hermit), which he never was in the strict interpretation of the term.

When but eighteen, the youthful Matteo left his native island, under the patronage of the good bishop, who loved him, to perfect his education in Rome, beneath the very shadow of St. Peter's, where he took holy orders at the early age of twenty-one. Then, according to his sad story, began that life of stormy passions and sorrowful pilgrimages, culminating in his assassination forty years afterwards in the far-off Occident.

He was called by the Church "Father Francesco," and although so young, was noted for his eloquence, subtile philosophy, and the boldness of his political utterances. But notwithstanding his pronounced views, the Pope named him as one of his secretaries. The College of the Propagandists, however, refused to confirm him, and placed him under interrogation and discipline. He eloquently defended himself, and the charges were not sustained. The severe discipline ended to which he had been subjected, and he was assigned to duty in the purlieus of the Eternal City.

In a short time, Matteo Boccalini's sunny nature and warm passions caused his disgrace. He became enamored of a fair devotee, one of his charge—a dark-haired, lustrous-eyed, bewitching creature of the "Land of the Vine." Alas! the too susceptible young priest succumbed to the wiles of the "radiant maiden," and he fell in a most earthly and fleshly way. Poor Boccalini was immediately and openly charged with the enormity of his crime, prosecuted, and denounced. He was despoiled of his sacerdotal functions, and compelled to flee; became a wanderer upon the face of the earth, supping with sorrow, and in despair for companions throughout the remainder of his mundane pilgrimage.

For a short time after his unwarranted and sinful escapade he campaigned with the heroic Garibaldi; then he turned with appealing looks toward America, the haven for all who are oppressed; crossed the ocean, and in a few weeks began his eventful journey on this continent. Never again was he to behold the place of his birth, the chalky outlines of fair, beautiful Capri, which so gloriously begems the Mediterranean. The phosphorescent Bay of Naples, the sky, the sunshine and vine-clad hills of dear old Italy, were never more to stir his once impulsive nature, or quicken into life his now deadened heart.

Years rolled on; youth passed by and middle

—3

age was upon the homeless priest, when, after
having roamed wearily from place to place, visiting one Indian tribe here and another there, in
the vain hope of discovering some clan, or people
near unto nature's heart, whose souls were at-
tuned to his own, who would receive him in the
simplicity of his severe and pious penance, he arrived among the Kaws, or Kansas, whose reservation was in the lovely valley of the Neosho, a few
miles below Council Grove. But that tribe, a
dirty, despicable race, very suspicious, and withal
not remarkable for their reverence of any religion, did not take kindly to the weary old man,
who had entered their midst with the purest intentions: his pious zeal, his abstinence and self-
denial made them fear to approach him. They
did not understand that—

> " When holy and devout religious men
> Are at their beads, 'tis hard to draw them thence,
> So sweet is zealous contemplation."

The miserable savages looked upon him, the
meek and humble pilgrim, as an intruder; said
he was "bad medicine." So Father Francesco
was no more at ease with them in their rude skin
lodges than he would have been in the gilded halls
of the Vatican.

He then came to Council Grove, as stated—

came as the tramp has since come, unheralded
and uninvited, but not to beg bread at the doors
of its residents, as the latter now does. Nor did
he come to tell off his beads in the presence of
the vulgar curious, but went upon the hillside
beyond the town, to seek the solitude and retire-
ment of a natural cave in the limestone rock of
the region, troubling no one; an enigma to the
world, and a subject for the idle gossip.

There for five months he lived, accessible to but
few, with whom, when he felt and recognized in
them the quickened glow of a soul that believed
in the Fatherhood of God and the Brotherhood of
Man, he would talk in tenderest strains of everything that was good, true, and beautiful.

The "hermit priest," as he was now called, had
of earthly possessions so little that he could have
vied with the lowly Nazarine in the splendor of
his poverty. Of crucifixes, devotional memen-
toes, and other religious trinkets, sweetly suggestive of better and happier days, he had preserved
a few. His greatest solace was in half a dozen
well-thumbed small volumes, between whose cov-
ers none peered but himself. He was ever regular
at his devotions; for notwithstanding he had
grievously sinned, as he declared, he was constantly striving to outlive its horrid memory, and

to repair the injury he had done his Master's cause.

He possessed one article of property that tinges his sojourn at Council Grove with a delightfully romantic remembrance among the very limited number now living there, who knew of the vagaries of the remarkably strange man; these were sometimes his confidants and friends, within a limited degree   It was a rudely constructed mandolin, which during all the years of his erratic pilgrimage he had tenaciously clung to, until its exterior presented a confused mass of scratches and dents, indicative of hard usage.   Despite all that, curious as it may seem, by some mysterious means its rich tones had been preserved in their original purity and depth.

On the evenings of Kansas' incomparable Indian summer, during the early part of which season he was living in his cave near Council Grove, the "hermit priest," seated on a projecting ledge at the mouth of his rocky and isolated retreat, would sweep the strings of his treasured instrument with a touch as light, deft, and sorrowfully tender as a maiden whose pure young heart had just been thrilled by its first breath of love.

To those who were so fortunate — and they were very few — as to be invited to spend an hour

with him, his vesper hymns, rendered in his ex-
quisite tenor voice, were as soul-inspiring as the
gentle earnestness of a young girl's prayer. His
sometime Neapolitan songs and soft airs of his
native isle were as sweet as the chant of the an-
gels he invoked when in a deeply religious mood,
and his heart-feeling tones mingled sadly with the
soughing of the evening breeze in the dense fo-
liage on the margin of the placid Neosho that
flowed near by. Thus, in the calm enjoyment of
his self-imposed solitude, he lived with

"The moss his bed, the cave his humble cell,
His food the fruits, his drink the crystal well."

Among the various languages necessary for the
communication of ideas between the motley crowd
comprising the civilization of the then remote ·
region, there was none that Matteo Boccalini did
not understand and speak fluently, so liberal had
been his education in that particular. ·

Once, when a stabbed and dying Mexican, the
victim of some gambling-quarrel among the drivers of the "bull-train" to which he was attached,
asked a service for the repose of his soul, Father
Francesco hastened to the anxious man's side.
There he administered the last sacrament of the
church to the expiring creature in his own lan-

guage, who died with a resigned look upon his
face, as he listened to the absolving words he
could perfectly understand, which was a thing of
joy to the holy man who had performed the sacred office.

One day late in the month of October, now
nearly thirty-six years ago, the "hermit priest"
saw walking through the streets of the little village a dark-visaged person, clad in clerical garb,
and whom Boccalini believed to be the lover of
the woman he had wronged in his youth, and that
the stranger, if it were he whom he suspected,
could never be persuaded to think that Matteo
was not wholly to be blamed for the life he had
blasted.

He told his friends he could no longer tarry
with them; he would go away to the mountains of
New Mexico, seek another cave, rear again the
blessed cross, emblem of his Master's suffering,
and once more live in solitude, from which he
had here somewhat strayed.

He frequently, when in a communicative mood,
had talked much to them of the delights of abso-
lute solitude. It was, he argued, the nurse of enthusiasm; that enthusiasm was the parent of
genius; that solitude had always been eagerly
sought for in every age; it was the inspiration of

the dominant religion of every nation; that their
founders were men who, seeking the quiet and seclusion of caverns or the desert, and subordinat-
ing the flesh to the spirit, had visions of the
"beyond." The veil hiding the better world had
been lifted for them, and their teachings had
come down to us through the æons, elevating man
above the brute.   •

The next morning after the sudden appearance
of the stranger whose presence had so discom-
posed the usually calm priest, a delicious morning in the month of "autumn's holocaust," when
the breeze was billowing the russet-colored grass
upon the virgin prairies, Father Francesco gathered up his few precious relics, and, accepting the
escort of a caravan just ready to start for New
Mexico, left Council Grove, his cave, and the
warm friends he had made there, forever.

The caravan under the protection of which the
frightened prelate went westward was owned by
a Mexican don, a brother-in-law to Kit Carson.
He still resides near the spot where the ill-fated
Italian, a year or two after his wearisome journey
across the Great Plains, was hurried to eternity.

This venerable Mexican and old-time voyageur
of the almost obliterated Santa Fé trail, when I
last visited him at his hospitable home in the

mountains, fourteen years ago, entertained me by relating some of the more prominent characteristics of his strange *compagnon du voyage* during that memorable trip with the "hermit priest" from Council Grove more than twenty years previously. He said that the strange man would never ride, either on horseback or in one of the wagons, despite the earnest invitation extended to him each recurring morning by the master of the caravan; preferring to trudge along uncomplainingly day after day during the sunny hours beside the plodding oxen through the alkali dust of the desert, and faltered not.

Neither would he at night partake of the shelter of a tent, constantly offered but as constantly and persistently refused, preferring to roll himself up in a single coarse wrap, seeking some quiet spot removed from the corral of wagons, where for an hour or two under the scintillating stars he would tell off his beads, or, accompanied by his mandolin, chant some sad refrain to the Virgin, until long after the camp had gone to sleep. For his subsistence he himself caught and cooked the prairie dog, ground squirrel, and gopher. Only occasionally, when hard pressed, would he accept a meal, which was constantly proffered by the Mexican teamsters, begging the "hermit

priest " to share with them; for in their love for
the Catholic Church, to which they were so devoted, he seemed to their untutored minds a most
zealous but humble exponent of their religious
tenets and visible form of their sacred faith.

Thus reticent, thoughtful and devout, he
marched with the caravan for many weeks, until
at last the city of Holy Faith, the quaint old
Spanish town of Santa Fé, was reached. There
he parted company with his escort, and for
nearly a year afterward wandered all over that
portion of the Territory of New Mexico, and into
Arizona, still seeking the Alnaschar of his dreams,
a suitable abiding-place in the recesses of the
hills, and a people whose souls might be made to
attune with his. But he miserably failed in all
that he desired during his sad pilgrimage throughout the Southwest. Then, turning northward
again, he slowly and almost despairingly retraced
his steps until he arrived in the sequestered valley
of the Sapillo, where he at last found a humble
class and his coveted cave on the summit of the
mighty mountain described at the opening of this
chapter.

There, content after so many years of unsatis-
fied wandering, he commenced that life of religious ministrations, and exercised those unselfish

acts of kindness and love, whose remembrance is imprinted so indelibly on the hearts of his devoted followers; for,

"Through suffering he soothed, and through sickness he nursed."

There again, under the constellations, which nowhere else shine more brilliantly, were the strains of his mandolin, and the rich notes of that magnificent voice, heard by the enchanted people who listened each evening at the doors of their rude adobe huts in the valley below the huge hill that cast its great shadow over them.

Notwithstanding the "hermit priest" had found a class congenial to his soul's demands, his eccentricities still clung to him. His persistency in living apart from his chosen people enforced them to always speak of him as "El Solitario" (The Solitary Man).

He would visit among them to solace and nurse the sick, and give absolution to the dying, which his and their religion so beautifully promises, but he would never break bread within their hospitable doors; preferring, and insisting, always, upon a crust and a cup of cold water outside.

Nor would he sleep upon the soft woolen *colchons* which even the poorest of New-Mexican homes afford, but, absorbed by devout thoughts, wrapped himself in his single coarse blanket and laid himself on the bare ground; or, if it was stormy, in some outhouse with the sheep and goats. This, of course, was part of his self-imposed penance, from which he never deviated, rigorous as it was.

One day, after his familiar and beloved face had been missed for more than a week by his devotees, a sorrowful party went out to seek him. They found him dead on the rugged trail to his lonely home; his beads enfolded in his delicately shaped fingers, and his countenance wearing a saint-like expression. A poisoned dagger in his heart, by the hand of an assassin, had accomplished the foul deed which for a whole lifetime, during every moment of the unhappy man's active and dreaming hours, was a continually disturbing fear.

Thus passed away, as he had predicted in his youth, the eccentric but holy Matteo Boccalini, "Hermit Priest" of the old "Santa Fé Trail," and the "El Solitario" of the New Mexico mountains. A man of sorrow and grief, yet with as much repentance, and as many penances as sins; one of those ethereal beings who might become physically unclean, but never spiritually impure.

For years after his departure from Council

Grove, the "hermit priest's" cave was an object
of much interest. Until within a very short
period, when the quarrymen tore down its last
vestige, upon its time-worn walls could be traced,
rudely carved, his name, "Matteo Boccalini," a
cross, "Jesu Maria," and "Capri"—all so dear
to the lonely and sad man's heart.

LITTLE BEAVER.

U NKNOWN, perhaps,. to the reader, in the very heart of the Wichita range, in the Indian Territory, there is an immense hill, which, by triangulation effected during the winter campaign of 1868–69 by the engineer officer attached to General Sheridan's headquarters, is three hundred. and ten feet high. At its base there is a clear, running river, or properly a creek — for it is only about seventy feet wide. The shape which the stream assumes. at the immediate foot of the mountain is that of a crescent, forming quite a large pool or basin.

Under the shadow which the great mass of dis-- rupted rock throws over the water at certain

hours, the pool looks as black as ink. The
moment the water emerges into the sunlight
again, it sparkles and scintillates until it is
painful for the eyes to rest upon its rapidly
flowing ripple. That the great elevation of this
detached portion of the range was caused by
some extraordinary convulsion, which moved it
from its normal position, is apparent, and curiosity is excited to assign a reason for the limited
area of the upheaval.

The stream which flows so picturesquely at the
base of the isolated mountain is called by the
Indians Medicine Bluff Creek; the hill above it,
Medicine Bluff. From the time when the memory of the various tribes "runneth not to the
contrary," Medicine Bluff has been a prominent
and sacred spot in the traditions and legitimate
history of the many nations of savages, but espe-
cially in that of the Comanches and Wichitas.
It was a sort of "Our Lady of Lourdes" place,
where the sick were cured in the most miraculous
manner after they had been given up by the celebrated doctors of the tribe. If the party afflicted
had never seriously grieved the Great Spirit, the
cure was as sudden as marvelous; if the sick,
who were carried to the top of the bluff by their
friends, had at any time offended the Great

Spirit, they died at once, the wolves devoured
their flesh, and their bones were transported to
the "Land of Terrors." Sometimes, when the
individual taken up to invoke the aid of the Indian god had lived an exemplary life, instead of
being cured of his fleshly ills he or she was trans-
lated, like Elisha of old, to the happy hunting-
grounds.

The Comanches declared that at night the Great
Spirit frequently rested on the top of the mountain, and when that occurred the whole region to
the verge of the horizon was lighted up with a
strange glow, resembling that emanating from an
immense prairie fire reflected upon the clouds.
The Indians also claimed that no dew or rain
ever fell upon the extreme summit of the bluff,
where the sick were to lie and wait for the manifestation of the Manitou; nor did the wind blow
there — so that it was a calm spot, comprising all
the essentials to a speedy recovery.

One among the many traditions connected with
the charming but weird place was told by an aged
warrior of the Comanches one evening, around
the camp-fire, in 1868, after white-winged Peace
had spread her wings once more over the prairies,
and we were pulling vigorously at our "brier-
woods" filled with fragrant "Lone Jack." The

old fellow, wrinkled and black with the smoke of the tepee in which he had lived for nearly eighty years, and now wrapped in that of his stone pipe, which he sucked as industriously as an infant, told this story:

There was once, ages before the white man had invaded the country of the Indian, a very old warrior, who, sick and despondent, went to the top of Medicine Bluff to be cured. He for many years had ceased to hunt the buffalo, lived with the women of the tribe, and settled himself down to a peaceful calm, awaiting the time when he should be called to join his fathers. One day he struggled to the top of the bluff in the hope that he might die and be carried bodily to the happy hunting-grounds, as he knew from the traditions of his tribe others had been before him.

He had been absent from his lodge and the village for three nights. During all that time the frightened people down below, who had been diligently watching, observed a great blaze on the top of the mountain, as if it were a signal-fire to warn them of some impending danger to the tribe.

On the third morning a young warrior was seen descending the trail from the heights of the bluff, drawing near to the village. When he entered its

streets he looked about him in evident surprise.
He approached the chief's lodge and sat down by
the fire.

The warriors of the tribe gazed at him with awe
and that curiosity which a stranger ever evokes.
No one seemed to recognize him. All remained
silent, waiting for him to speak. Lighting his
pipe with a coal, he took a pull at it himself,
Indian fashion, then passed it around the circle.
The warriors noticed that his pipe-stem was deco-
rated with the feathers of the gray eagle, denoting
him to be a great warrior, one who had captured
a large number of scalps, so they regarded him
with still greater wonder. After every one in the
circle around the chief's fire had taken a whiff,
the stranger commenced his story:

"After I arrived at the top of the Medicine
Bluff, I looked off at the vast expanse which
surrounded me. I saw the village of my people;
I could hear the dogs bark and the children
laugh; I could hear my own family mourning,
as if some one had been taken from them; I saw
the buffalo covering the prairie, and the cunning wolf lying in wait to pounce upon his prey.
When I again looked all around me, and beheld
the young warriors in their pride and strength, I
asked myself: 'Why do I live any longer? My

. —4

fires have gone out. I must follow my fathers. The world is beautiful to the young, but to the old it has no pleasure. I will go there!'

"With this upon my mind, I continued: 'Far away toward the setting sun are the hunting-grounds of my people.' Then I gathered all my strength and leaped from the giddy height before me. I knew no more of the woes of this life. I was caught up in mid-air and suddenly transported to a country where game was countless; where there was no wind, no rain, no sickness; where all the great chiefs of the Comanches who had ever died were assembled; where they were all young again, and chased the buffalo and feasted as when on earth. There was no darkness. The people were continually happy. Beautiful birds sang on the trees. The war-whoop was never more heard."

The old chief had been rejuvenated, and now came back to his people with all his youthful vigor, to live again with his own tribe. The story of the strange warrior captivated the Indians.

He at once became an oracle and great medicine-man in his tribe; his power to cure the sick was wonderful, and his counsel was implicitly obeyed ever afterward.

Medicine Bluff has of course lost much of its prestige among the Indians, for the reason that since the extinction of the buffalo and other large game the tribes have been scattered, being generally pretty closely confined to the reservations, with the children taught in schools, and the superstitions, or at least many of them, having passed gradually out of the remembrance of the new generation, known only to the few old warriors left.

The savage, like the white man, in his disappointments and miseries sometimes resorts to suicide as a cure-all for and end-all of life's burdens. Among the powerful Comanches Medicine Bluff was, for an unknown period, one of their famous places, like the Vendome Column in Paris, from which to terminate an unsatisfactory and miserable existence. The bluff was also a rendezvous for the young warriors, who were to go for the first time in battle with the tried soldiers of the tribe, to propitiate the Great Spirit.

The sun in that nation, as in the old tribe of Natchez, symbolized their god. For three consecutive mornings the youthful aspirant for military honors was obliged to go to the highest point of the great hill, where, armed with his buffalo

hide, and alone, he was with the utmost reverence to present the front of his shield' to the
early morning sun as its rays gilded the rocky
crags of the mountain, assuming the attitude of
a warrior in the heat of battle, on guard against
his enemy's spear and shower of arrows. This
ceremony on the part of the novitiate, if rever-
ently performed, gave his shield invulnerable
power.

A story told to many of . us during the campaign referred to, by one of the oldest of the
Comanches, the oldest Indian I have ever seen —
" Little Beaver," of the Osages — is very interesting, showing to what an art the despised savage
of thirty years ago reduced story-telling. The
dried-up old warrior prefaced his tale by stating
that he was so aged "that he was brother of the
highest peak of the Wichita Mountains," at the
foot of which we were camped on a cold December night in 1868. Here is the story:

So many years ago that it seemed like a dream
even to the narrator, the Comanches were the
greatest tribe on earth. Their warriors were as
numerous as a herd of buffalo on the Arkansas
in the fall. They were more cunning than the
coyote. Their herd of ponies contained so many
animals — all fine and fat — that no man could

count them in a year. All the other Indians of
the plains and mountains feared and trembled at
the name of Comanche.

In the tribe, as is ever the case, there were
two warriors who excelled all the others in their
prowess. One was young, and the other middle-
aged. They were very jealous of each other, each
constantly attempting some deed of daring at
which, it was hoped, the rival would balk. One
fall, when the Indian summer made the air red-
olent with the sweet perfume of thousands of
flowers and the mountains were bathed in the
amber mist of that delicious season, all the great
warriors were returning from one of their most
famous victories.

They camped under the shadow of Medicine
Bluff late one afternoon, where the young brave,
who was quietly smoking his pipe as he hovered
over the little camp-fire on which he was broiling
a piece of antelope steak, happened to fix his
gaze on the highest point of the bluff, and in that
position continued for several minutes wrapped
in a most profound study, while all the rest of
the band stopped whatever they were doing and
gazed at him as intently.

Suddenly he rose to his full height and cast a
defiant look upon the warriors scattered around

on the grass, who, excited at his strange manner, sprang up to learn what he meant. Presently he turned his face toward the sun, which was about two hours high, and broke out with this boast:

"No warrior equals me! I am the greatest of all the Comanches! I resemble that mountain!" pointing with his spear to the highest peak of Medicine Bluff. "My actions are as far above yours as that mountain is above the stream at its foot! Is there a warrior here who dare follow me?"

Then he shook his spear and brandished his shield in defiance of any and all. His rival was all the time swelling with rage and pride. He knew the boast was intended for him alone, although he was the elder of the two. He approached the braggart with all the dignity of the savage that he was, and, striking himself on the bosom several times, exclaimed:

"So! You are the greatest warrior of the Comanches? You are the buffalo that leads the herd? I am the old bull to be driven away by the cowardly coyote and die, leaving my bones to whiten? You ask me to follow you? Never! I never follow! I will go with you!"

The remainder of the band gathered around the two celebrated warriors. They wondered what new deed of daring they were going to attempt, as the rivals arrayed themselves in their best buckskin dress and mounted their favorite ponies. With shields held in a defying position, their faces painted, and their bonnets of war-eagle feathers flowing in the breeze, they rode away without another word.

They forded the stream. The younger now started up the difficult trail which led to the sacred summit of the Medicine Bluff, where, stopping his affrighted steed, he pointed to the fearful precipice a few rods off, and exclaimed:

"You have followed me here; follow me farther."

Then shouting the war-whoop, which made the echoes of the mountain awaken, and thumping

the flanks of his animal vigorously, he darted toward the awful brink. His rival instantly raised his pony on his hind legs, and with a whoop more piercing followed the young man, who, when he had reached the edge of the precipice, failed in-courage and pulled his pony violently back on his haunches. The elder saw his chance. With an awful yell of defiance and triumph, he forced his horse to make the terrible leap in mid-air.

All the warriors on the grassy bottom below watched with eager interest what was going on above them. They heard the whoop of the aged warrior as he jumped into the awful abyss. They saw him sit as calmly as if in his "lodge" as he descended, seated as upright on his pony as if his animal were walking the prairie, and, above all, they heard his clear voice as it rung out in the clouds: "Greatest of all the Comanches !"

Sadly they wended their way to the foot of the bluff, where both horse and brave rider lay a mangled mass on the rocks, the old warrior with a smile on his wrinkled face of unmistakable triumph.

The boasting rival became a wanderer among the tribes. His name was accursed of all Indians.

The very dogs of the camps snapped at him as he passed. At last, overcome with remorse at his cowardice and treachery, he killed himself. One day he was found dead on the grave of his rival at the foot of the bluff. His body was eaten by the coyotes; his shield and spear, by which he had been identified, were lying on the ground at his feet.

A RACE FOR LIFE.

AN INCIDENT OF THE INDIAN WAR OF 1864.

KICKING BIRD.

I N 1864 the magnificent valley of the "Smoky Hill," with its rich share of wooded streams and fertile uplands, and the still more Elysian expanse watered by the great Arkansas—that embryo granary of two continents — were simply known as the region through which passed twin inter-oceanic trails, the Oregon and the Santa Fé, both now mere memories.

The commerce of the Great Plains over that broad path through the wilderness, the Santa Fé Trail, was at its height, and immense trains rolled day after day toward the blue hills which guard the portals of New Mexico. Oxen, mules, and sometimes horses, tugged wearily week after week through the monotony of their long journey, their precious freight ever tempting the wily nomads to plunder, dissimulation, and murder. Pawnee Rock, Walnut, Coon, Ash and Cow creeks were mute witnesses of a score or more battles that reddened the blossoming prairie in springtime, and the slopes of the Pawnee, Heath's Branch and Buckner's were resonant with the yell of the Kiowa and Cheyenne, who under the pale moonlight held their hideous saturnalia of butchery.

To protect the trains on their weary route through the "desert"—as the whole of this region was then termed, and confidently believed by the world to be—troops were stationed, a mere handful, relatively, at intervals on the "great trail," to escort the freighters and the United States mail over the most exposed and dangerous portions of the route.

The incident which is the subject of this sketch is as thrilling, perhaps, in its details, and as marvelous in its results, as any that have come down to us in the history of those memorable times. It deals with plain facts, and men who are now living—one of whom, the principal actor in the scenes to be related, is known favorably all over the State. [Capt. Henry Booth, just passed away —1898.]

Fort Riley, in the year referred to, was one of

the extreme permanent military posts. Here, in November, 1864, Capt. Henry Booth was stationed. He was chief of cavalry and inspecting officer for the district of the Upper Arkansas, the western geographical limit of which extended to the foot of the Rocky Mountains.

Early in the month, in company with Lieut. Hallowell, of the Ninth Wisconsin Battery, he received orders to make a tour of inspection of the several outposts, which extended as far as Fort Lyon, in Colorado.

Salina was occupied by one company of the Seventh Iowa Cavalry, under command of Capt. Hammer. Where the old Leavenworth stage route crossed the Smoky Hill, in a beautifully timbered bend of that stream, was a little log stockade, commanded by Lieut. Ellsworth, also of the Seventh Cavalry.

To this comparatively insignificant post — insignificant only in its appointments, not in importance — the commanding officer gave his own name, which the county of Ellsworth will perpetuate in history.

At the crossing of the Walnut, on the broad trail to the mountains, were stationed three hundred unassigned recruits of the Third Wisconsin Cavalry, under the command of Capt. Conkey.

This was one of the most important points of observation on the "Great Overland Route," for near it passed the favorite highway of the Indians on their yearly migrations north and south.

This primitive cantonment grew rapidly in its strategic aspect, was later made quite formidable, defensively, and was named Fort Zarah in memory of the youngest son of Maj. Gen. Curtis, killed by guerrillas somewhere south of Fort Scott, while escorting Gen. James G. Blunt, of Kansas fame.

At Fort Larned, always a prominent point in the military history of the Plains, one company of the Twelfth Kansas and a section of the Ninth Wisconsin Battery commanded by Lieut. Potter were stationed. From these troops — the isolated disposition of which I have hurriedly related — squads, consisting usually of from a dozen to twenty men or more, as the case might be, under the charge of a corporal or sergeant, were detailed to escort the mail coach, freighters, Government trains, etc.

On the morning the order (to make the special inspection of the outposts referred to) was received at Fort Riley, Captain Booth and Lieut. Hallowell immediately commenced active preparations for their extended and hazardous drive across the prairies.

All preliminaries arranged, the question as to the means of transportation of the two officers was determined in this wise, and as the sequel will show, curiously enough saved the lives of the two heroes in the terrible gauntlet they were destined to run.

Lieut. Hallowell was a famous "whip," and prided himself upon his exceptionally fine turnout which he daily drove around the picturesque hills of Fort Riley.

"Booth," said he that morning, "let's not take a great lumbering ambulance on this trip. If you will get a good team of mules from the quartermaster, I will furnish my light wagon, and we will do our own driving."

"All right," replied Booth; "I'll get the mules."

Lieut. Hallowell therefore had a set of bows fitted to his light rig, over which was thrown an army wagon-sheet, drawn up behind with a cord, similar to the fashion of the average emigrant outfit now so often to be seen upon the roads of our Western prairies. A round hole was thus left at the end, which served as a window, and as will be seen further on, played a most important part in the tragedy in which this simply covered wagon figured so conspicuously.

Two valises containing their dress uniforms, a box of crackers and cheese, meat and sardines, and a bottle of anti-snakebite, made up the precious freight for the long journey; and in the clear cold of the early morning they rolled out of the gates of the fort, escorted by Company L of the Eleventh Kansas, commanded by Lieut. Jacob Van Antwerp.

Junction City was in those days in reality the limit of civilization, although Abilene with its solitary log cabin, and Salina with only two, made great pretensions as the most westerly cities of the Great Plains. A single glance at the howling wilderness surrounding either place, however, dissipated all idea of possible or probable future metropolitan greatness.

The rough bluffs that border Alum and Clear creeks, in Ellsworth county, through which the trail wound its tortuous way, were always in those days a favorite haunt of the Indians, and many a solitary straggler has met his death from their swift arrows in what are now called the "Harker Hills."

Safely through these dangerous bluffs and across the beautiful bottoms that are to-day dotted with some of the most picturesque homes in Ellsworth county, marched the little army and its one white covered ambulance. Not an incident disturbed the quiet of the grand autumn day, except the occasional slaughter of buffalo in mere wantonness now and then by some straggling soldier; and early in the afternoon the stockade in the bend of the Smoky Hill was reached.

After an inspection of this remote little garrison, which was found in excellent spirits and condition, the line of march was resumed next morning for Capt. Conkey's camp on the Walnut.

The company of 100 men acting as an escort were too formidable a number to invite the cupidity of the Indians, and not a sign of one was seen as the dangerous flats of Plum creek and the rolling country beyond were successively passed; and the cantonment on the Walnut was reached with nothing to disturb the monotony of the march.

Capt. Conkey's command at this important outpost were living in a rude but comfortable sort of way in the simplest of dugouts constructed along the bank of the stream, and the officers, a little more in accordance with military dignity, in tents a few rods to the rear of the line of huts. A stockade stable had been built, with a capacity of two hundred and fifty horses, and sufficient hay had been put up by the men to carry the horses through the winter.

The Captain was a brusque but kind-hearted man, and with him were stationed his other officers, one of whom was a son of Admiral Goldsborough, of naval fame.

The next morning Capt. Booth made a rigid inspection of the place, which took all day, as an immense amount of property had accumulated for condemnation ; and when evening came, the papers, books, etc., were still untouched, and this branch of the inspection was postponed until the morning.   In the evening while sitting around the campfire, discussing the war, telling stories, etc., Capt. Conkey said to Booth : "Captain, it won't take more than half an hour in the morning to inspect the papers and finish up what you have got to do : why don't you start your escort out early ?—then they won't be obliged to trot after the ambulance, or you to poke along with them.   You can then move out briskly and make time."

Acting upon this suggestion, Capt. Booth went over the creek to Lieut. Van Antwerp's camp and told him he need not wait for the ambulance in the morning, but to march at about half-past six or at seven o'clock, in advance.   So at daylight the escort marched out agreeably to instructions, and Booth continued his inspection.   It was

—5

found, however, that either Capt. Conkey had misjudged the amount of work to be done or the inspecting officer's ability to do it in a certain time, and nearly three hours elapsed before the task was completed.

At last everything was closed up, much to the satisfaction of Lieut. Hallowell, who had been chafing under the delay ever since the troops departed. When all was in readiness and the ambulance drawn up in front of the commanding officer's tent, Lieut. Hallowell suggested to Booth the propriety of taking a few of the men stationed there with them until they overtook their own escort, which must now be several miles on the trail toward Fort Larned. So, upon this, Booth mentioned it to Capt. Conkey, who said: "Oh, there is no danger; there hasn't an Indian been seen around here for more than ten days."

If they had known as much about Indians then as they afterward learned, Capt. Conkey's response, instead of assuring them, would have made them insist upon an escort, which Booth in his official capacity had the power to order; but they were satisfied, and concluded to push on. Jumping into the wagon, Lieut. Hallowell took the lines, and away they went, rattling over the old log bridge that used to span the Walnut, as light of heart as if riding to a dance. It was a clear cold morning, with a stiff breeze blowing from the northwest; their trail was frozen hard in some places, and was very rough, caused by the travel of heavy trains when it was wet.

Booth sat on the left side with the whip in his hand, occasionally striking the animals to keep their speed. Hallowell struck up a tune (he was a good singer), and Booth joined in as they rolled along, as oblivious of danger as though they were in their quarters at Riley.

After they had proceeded some distance, Hallowell remarked, "The buffalo are grazing a long distance from the road to-day—a circumstance which I think bodes no good." He had been on the Plains the summer before, and was better acquainted with the Indians and their peculiarities than Capt. Booth; but the latter replied that he "thought it was because their escort had gone along ahead, and had probably frightened them away." The next mile or two was passed, and still they saw no buffalo between the trail and the river; but nothing more was said relative to the suspicious circumstance, and they rolled rapidly on.

When about five or six miles from Zarah, on glancing toward the river, to the left and front,

Booth saw something that looked strangely like a
drove of turkeys; he watched them intently for a
few minutes, when they rose up, and he discovered they were horsemen. He grasped Hallowell's
left arm, and directed his attention to them, say-
ing, "What's that?" Hallowell cast a hasty
look to the point indicated, and replying, "Indians, by George!" immediately turned the mules
and started them back toward Fort Zarah on a
full gallop.

"Hold on," said Booth; "maybe it is a part
of our escort."

"No, no," replied Hallowell; "I know it's Indians."

"Well," replied Booth, "I am going to see;"
so, stepping out on the footboard and holding
onto the front bow, he looked back over the top
of the wagon. There was no doubt now that they
were Indians. They had fully emerged from the
ravines in which they were hidden, and while he
was looking were slipping their buffalo robes from
their shoulders, taking arrows out of their quiv-
ers, drawing up their spears, and making ready
generally for a red-hot time. While Booth was
intently watching their hostile movements, Hallowell asked, "They are Indians, aren't they?"

"Yes," replied Booth, "and they are coming
like blazes!"

"Oh, dear!" said Hallowell, in a despairing
tone; "I shall never see poor Lizzie again." He
had been married for only a few weeks, and his
young wife's name was Lizzie.

"Never mind Lizzie," said Booth; "let's get
out of here!" Although he was as badly frightened as Hallowell, he had no bride at Riley, and
as he tells it, "was selfishly thinking of himself
and escape."

Promptly in response to Booth's remark came
back from Hallowell in a firm voice, clear and
determined as ever issued from mortal throat:
"All right; you do the shooting and I'll do the
driving," and suiting the action to the word, he
snatched the whip out of Booth's hand, slipped
from the seat to the front of the wagon and commenced lashing the mules.

Booth then crawled back, pulled one of his revolvers—he had two, Hallowell only one—then
crept, or rather fell, over the "lazy-back" of the
seat, reached the hole made by the puckering of
the sheet, and counted the Indians. Thirty-four
feather‑bedecked, paint‑bedaubed savages, as
vicious-looking an outfit as ever scalped a white
man, were coming down upon them like a hawk
upon a chicken.

Booth had hardly reached his place at the back

of the wagon before Hallowell, between his yells
to the mules, cried out, "How far off are they
now, Cap.?"—for he could see nothing in the
rear as he sat.

Booth answered him as well as he could, and
Hallowell renewed his lashing and yelling.

Noiselessly the Indians gained, for as yet they
had not uttered a whoop.

Again Hallowell asked, "How far off are they
now, Cap.?" and again Booth gave him an idea
of the distance between them and their merciless
foe. From him Hallowell gathered fresh inspiration for fresh yells and still more vigorous blows.

Booth was sitting on a box containing crackers, sardines, etc., watching the approach of the
cut-throats, and saw with fear and trembling the
ease with which they gained upon the little
wagon. He realized then that safety did not
lie in flight alone, and that something besides
mules' heels would be necessary to preserve their
scalp-locks.

Once more Hallowell inquired the distance between the pursued and pursuing, but before Booth
could answer, two shots were fired by the rifles
from the Indians, accompanied by a yell that
was enough to make the blood curdle in one's
veins, and no reply was needed to acquaint the

valorous driver that the fiends were sufficiently
near to commence making trouble. He yelled at
the mules, and down came the whip upon the
poor animals' backs. Booth yelled, for what reason he did not know, unless to keep company
with Hallowell, while the wagon flew over the
rough road like a patent baby-jumper. The bullets from the two rifles passed through the wagon-
cover immediately between the officers, but did
no damage; and almost instantly the Indians
charged down upon them, dividing into two parties, one going on each side, and delivering a volley
of arrows into the wagon as they rode by.

Just as they darted past the mules, Hallowell
cried out, "Cap., I'm hit!" and turning around
to look at him, Booth saw an arrow sticking in
his head above his right ear; his arm was still
plying the whip, which was going as unceasingly
as the sails of a windmill, and his yelling only
stopped long enough to answer, "Not much," in
response to Booth's "Does it hurt?" as he grabbed the arrow and pulled it out of his head.

The Indians by this time had passed on, and
then, circling back, prepared for another charge.

Booth had already fired at them three or four
times, but owing to the distance, the jumping of
the wagon, and the "unsteadiness of his nerves,"

as he declared, the shots had not decreased to any
material extent the number of their assailants.

Down came the red devils again, dividing as before, and delivering another lot of arrows. Hallowell stopped yelling long enough to cry out,
" I'm hit again, Cap.! "

Looking around, Booth saw an arrow sticking
in Hallowell's head, just over his left ear this
time, and hanging down his back like an orna-
ment. He snatched it out, asked Hallowell if it
hurt him, but received the same answer as before
—"No; not much."

Both were yelling at the top of their voices,
the mules were jerking the wagon along at a fearful rate—frightened nearly out of their wits at
the sight of the Indians and the shouting and
whipping of their drivers. Booth, crawling to
the back end of the wagon again and looking
out, saw the Indians moving across the trail,
preparing for another charge. One old fellow
mounted on a black pony was jogging along in
the center of the road behind them, quite near,
and evidently intent on sending an arrow through
the puckered hole of the wagon-sheet. As Booth
looked out, the Indian stopped his pony and let
fly. Booth dodged back sideways; the arrow sped
on in its course, and came whizzing through the

hole and struck the black-walnut "lazy-back" of
the seat, the head sticking entirely through, the
sudden checking causing the feathered end to vi-
brate rapidly with a vro-o-o-ing sound. With a
sudden blow Booth struck it, breaking the shaft
from the head, leaving the latter imbedded in the
wood.

As quick as he could, Booth rushed to the hole
and fired at his aged opponent, but failed to hit
him. While he was trying to get another shot at
him, an arrow came flying from the left side, and
struck him on the inside of the elbow, hitting the
nerve or "crazy-bone," which so benumbed his
hand and arm that he could not hold on to his
revolver, and it dropped from his hand to the
road with one load still in its chamber. Just
then the mules gave an extra jump, which nearly
jerked the wagon from under him, and he fell on
the end-gate, evenly balanced, with his hands
sprawling outside, attempting to clutch at something to save himself.

At this the Indians gave a terrible yell — of
exultation, probably, supposing Booth was going
to fall out; but he didn't. He caught hold of
one of the wagon-bows and pulled himself in
again, terribly scared. It was a "close call"
and no mistake!

While all this was going on, Hallowell had not been neglected by the incarnate fiends; about a dozen of them had devoted their time and attention to him, but he had not flinched. Just as Booth had regained his equilibrium and drawn the second revolver from his holster, Hallowell yelled, "Right off to the right, Cap.—quick!"

Booth tumbled over the back of the seat, clutching at a bow to steady himself, and "right off to the right" was an Indian just letting fly at Hallowell. The arrow struck the side of the wagon; Booth at the instant fired at the Indian, missed him of course—but he was badly scared, and throwing himself on the opposite side of his pony, scooted off over the prairie.

Back over the seat Booth piled again to guard the rear, where he found a young buck riding close behind and to the right of the wagon, his pony following the trail made by the ox-drivers in walking beside their teams. Putting his arm around one of the wagon-bows, to prevent being jerked out, Booth quickly stuck his revolver through the hole; but before he could fire, the Indian flopped over on the side of his pony, and all that could be seen of him was his arm around the pony's neck, and from the knee down, one leg. Booth did not fire, but waited for him to come up — he could almost hit the pony's head with his hand, so closely was he running. He struck at it several times, but the Indian kept him close up by whipping him on the opposite side of his neck. Presently the Indian's arm began to work, and Booth looking saw that he had fixed an arrow in his bow behind the pony's shoulder, and was just on the point of shooting at him, with the head of the arrow not three feet from his breast as he leaned out of the hole in the wagon-sheet. Booth struck frantically at the arrow and dodged back into the wagon. Up came the Indian, but Booth went out again, for he realized that the Indian had to be gotten away from there, as he would make trouble. Whenever Booth went out, down went the Indian; up he rose in a moment again, but Booth fearing to risk himself with his head and breast exposed at this game of "hide-and-seek," drew back as the Indian went down the third time, and in a second up he came again — but this was once too often. Booth had only gotten partly in and had not dropped his revolver, and as the Indian rose, instinctively, and without taking aim, fired.

The ball struck the Indian in the left nipple (he was naked to the waist), the blood spurted out of the wound almost to the wagon, his bow

and arrow and lariat-rope dropped, he fell back
on the pony's rump and rolled from there heavily onto the ground, where, after a convulsive
straightening of his legs and a characteristic
"Ugh!" he lay as quiet as a stone.

"I've killed one of them, Hallowell!" yelled
out Booth, as the Indian tumbled off his pony.

"Bully for you!" came back the response; and
then he continued his shouting, and the blows of
that tireless whip fell incessantly upon the mules.

All the Indians that were in the rear and saw
the young warrior fall, rode up to him, circling
around his dead body, uttering the most unearthly yells,—but different from anything they
had given vent to before.

Hallowell, from his cramped position in front,
noticed the change in their tone, and asked, "What
are they doing now, Cap.?"

Booth explained to him, and Hallowell's response was more vociferous yelling and harder
blows upon the poor galloping mules.

Booth was still sitting on the cracker-box,
watching the maneuvers of the Indians, when
suddenly Hallowell sang out, " Right off to the
right, Cap.—quick!" which startled him, and
whirling around instantly, he saw an Indian
within three feet of the wagon, with his bow

and arrow almost ready to shoot. There was no
time to get over the seat, and as he could not fire
by Hallowell, he cried out, "Hit him with the
whip! Hit him with the whip!" The lieutenant,
suiting the action to the word, simply diverted
one of the blows intended for the mules, and
struck the Indian fair across the face.

The whip had a knot on the end of it to keep it
from unraveling, and this knot must have hit the
Indian in the eye, for he dropped his bow, put his
hands up to his face, rubbed his eyes, and digging
his heel into the left side of his pony, was soon
out of reach of a revolver, but nevertheless he was
given a parting shot — a sort of salute, for it was
harmless.

A terrific yell from the rear at this moment
caused Booth to look around, and Hallowell to
inquire, "What's the matter now?" "They are
coming down upon us like lightning!" replied
Booth; and sure enough, those who had been
prancing around their dead comrade were coming
toward the wagon like a whirlwind, and with a
whoop more deafening and hideous than any that
had preceded it.

Hallowell yelled louder than ever and lashed
the mules more furiously still, but the Indians
gained on them as easily as a blooded racer on a

common farm plug. Separating as before, and
passing on each side of the wagon, the Indians
delivered another volley as they charged by.

As this charge was made, Booth drew away
from the hole in the rear of the wagon-cover
and turned his seat toward the Indians, but for-
got in the moment of excitement that, in the
manner that he was sitting, his back pressed
against the sheet, his body probably plainly out-
lined on the outside.

When the Indians rushed by and delivered their
storm of arrows, Hallowell cried out, "I'm hit
again, Cap.!" and Booth, in turning around to
go to his relief, felt something pulling at him.
Glancing over his left shoulder to learn the cause
of his trouble, he discovered an arrow sticking
into him and out through the wagon-sheet. With
a jerk of his body he tore it loose, and going to
Hallowell, asked, "Where are you hit now?"
"In the back," he answered; where on looking
Booth saw an arrow sticking, the shaft extending
under the "lazy-back" of the seat. Taking hold
of it, he gave it a pull, but Hallowell squirmed so
that he desisted. "Pull it out! Pull it out!"
he cried. Booth thereupon took hold of it again,
and, giving a jerk or two, out it came. He was
thoroughly frightened as he saw it leave the lieu-

tenant's body, for it seemed to have entered at
least six inches, and looked as if it must have
made a dangerous wound; but Hallowell did not
cease belaboring the mules, and his yells, accompanied by the blows, rang out as clear as before.

After pulling out the arrow, Booth turned again
to the opening at the rear of the wagon, to see
what new tricks the miscreants were up to, when
Hallowell yelled again, "Right off to the left,
Cap.— quick ! "

Rushing to the front of the wagon as soon as
possible, Booth saw an Indian in the act of shooting at the lieutenant from the left side, and about
ten feet away. The last revolver was empty, but
something had to be done at once; so, leveling the
weapon at him, Booth yelled, "Bang ! you son-
of-a-gun ! "

Down went the Indian; rap, rap, went his knees
against his pony's sides, and away he flew over
the prairie.

Back over the seat Booth tumbled, and began
to load his revolver. The cartridges they had in
those days were the old-fashioned paper kind,
and biting off the end of one he would endeavor
to pour the powder into the chamber, but the
wagon was tumbling from side to side and jumping up and down as it flew over the rough trail,.

and more of the powder went into the bottom of the wagon than into the revolver.

Just as he was inserting a ball in the chamber, Hallowell cried out again, "Right off to the left, Cap.—quick!" Over the seat Booth went once more, and there was another Indian, with his bow and arrow in his hand, all ready to plug the lieutenant. Pointing his revolver at him, Booth yelled as he had at the other, but the Indian had evidently noticed the failure to fire at the first, and concluded that there were no more loads left; so, instead of taking a hasty departure as his comrade had done, he grinned a demoniacal grin and endeavored to fix the arrow into his bow.

Thoroughly frightened now at the aspect things were assuming, Booth rose up in the wagon, and grasping hold of a bow with his left hand, seized the revolver by the muzzle, and with all the force he could muster, hurled it at the impudent brute. It was a new Remington octagon barrel, with sharp corners, and when it was thrown turned in the air, striking the Indian, muzzle first, on the ribs, cutting a long gash.

"Ugh!" grunted the Indian, and dropping his long spear and bow, he flung himself over the side of the pony, and away he went over the prairie, to bother them no more.

Only the one revolver left now, and that empty, and the Indians still howling around the apparently doomed men like so many demons.

After he had driven the Indian off, Booth fell over the seat, picked up the empty revolver and attempted to load; but before he could bite off a cartridge, Hallowell yelled again, " I'm hit again, Cap.!"

"Where are you hit now?" asked the gallant captain.

"In the hand," replied Hallowell.

Looking around, Booth saw his right arm was plying the whip to the now laggard mules, and sticking through the fleshy part of his thumb was an arrow, which was flopping up and down as his arm rose and fell in its ceaseless and evidently tireless efforts to keep up the speed of the almost exhausted animals.

"Let me pull it out," said Booth.

"No, never mind," said Hallowell; "can't stop, can't stop"—and up and down went his arm, and flip-flap went the arrow with it, until finally it tore through the flesh and fell to the ground.

Along they bowled, the Indians yelling and the occupants of the wagon defiantly answering them, while Booth was still making a desperate but vain

—6

effort to load the revolver. In a few moments
Hallowell shouted, "They are crowding the mules
into the sunflowers!"

Along the sides of the trail huge sunflowers had
grown the previous summer, and now their dry
stalks stood as thick as a canebrake, and if the
wagon once got among them the mules could not
keep up their gallop, and would soon be compelled
to stop.

The Indians seemed to realize this fact, and one
huge fellow kept riding beside the off mule and
throwing his spear at him and then jerking it
back with the thong, one end of which was fastened to his wrist, the other to the shaft of the
spear. The mule on the side next the Indian was
jumping frantically and pushing the near mule
from the road.

Stepping out on the footboard, and holding a
bow with one hand, Booth commenced kicking
the mule vigorously. Hallowell, meanwhile, was
pulling on one line, whipping and yelling; so together they forced the animals back into the
trail, and away they shot at the top of their
speed.

The Indian kept close to the mules, and Booth
made several attempts to scare him by pointing
his revolver at him; but he would not scare, so

he threw it at him. It missed the Indian, but
struck the pony just behind the rider's leg, which
started the latter off over the prairie, thus remov-
ing the immediate peril from that source.

They were now absolutely without firearms—
nothing left but their sabers and valises; and the
Indians, soon learning that there were no more
shots to be fired, came closer and closer.

In turn the two sabers were thrown at them, as
they came almost within striking distance; then
followed the scabbards after the yelling fiends, as
they surrounded the wagon. Some rode immediately in front of the mules, impeding their
progress with the most infernal noises and attempts to spear them (the Indians having evidently exhausted all their arrows)—and the
camp on the Walnut still a mile and a half
away.

There was nothing left for our luckless travelers to do but whip and kick the mules and yell,
all of which they did most lustily—Hallowell
sitting as immovable as a sphinx, except his right
arm, which from the time he had started had not
ceased, and Booth kicking the poor animals and
shouting in concert with their importunate foe.
Looking casually over the seat, Booth saw twelve
or fifteen Indians coming up behind, with their

spears all unstrung and ready for action, and he felt that something must be done, and that right speedily, to divert them; for if these were added to the number already surrounding the wagon, the chances were they would succeed in forcing the mules from the trail, and the end of the tragedy would soon come.

Glancing around the bottom of the wagon, in his despair, for some kind of weapon with which to resist them, Booth's eye rested upon the valises containing the dress suits, and snatching his, threw it out, while his pursuers were yet some four or five rods behind. The Indians noticed these new tricks with a yell of apparent satisfaction, and as soon as they reached the valise they all dismounted, and one of them grabbed it by the two handles and attempted to open it; failing in this, another drew a long knife from under his blanket, and, ripping up one side, thrust in his hand and pulled out a sash, and began winding it around his head (as a negro woman winds a bandana), letting the tassels hang down his back.

While he was thus amusing himself, another had pulled out a dress coat, a third a pair of drawers, still another a shirt—all of which they individually proceeded to put on, meanwhile dancing around and yelling.

Booth reported to Hallowell how the sacrifice
of his valise had diverted the Indians, and said,
"I'm going to throw out yours."

"All right," he replied; "let her go; all we
want is time." So out it went, and shared the
same fate as the other.

As long as the Indians were busy helping themselves to the wardrobes contained in the two valises, they were not bothering the mules, and as
Hallowell had said, "all they wanted was time."

But while the diversion was going on in the
rear, the devils on each side and front were still
attempting to force the mules from the road by
rushing at them and yelling, and brandishing
their spears; none of them had as yet tried to
kill them, evidently thinking they could wound
the two officers and secure them alive—a prize
too valuable for an Indian to lose. But as they
were now drawing near the creek, on the opposite
bank of which the camp was situated, and the
chance of escape grew brighter, one miserable cut-
throat of the band apparently conceived the idea
of killing one of the mules, for he charged down
on the wagon, rode close up to one, and discharg-
ing his arrow at him, struck him on the fore leg,
severing a small artery, from which the blood
spurted by jerks. The mules had no blinds on

their bridles, and the one hurt, seeing the blood, became so frightened that he gave a terrific jump and started off at a break-neck gait, dragging the other mule and the wagon after him; so all the occupants had now to do was to pound and kick the uninjured one to make him keep up.

This fresh spurt of speed had carried them away from the Indians, but Booth and Hallowell knew that the animals could not continue it, and they became convinced that the Indians now meant to kill one or both of the mules in order to stop them.

The lull caused by the mules outstripping the Indians gave our almost despairing heroes time to talk the matter over.

Hallowell said he did not propose to be captured and taken to Medicine Lodge creek, or some other place, and then butchered or burned at the leisure of the Indians. He said to Booth, "If they kill a mule and we stop, let's kick, strike, throw clods or anything, and compel them to kill us on the spot." So they agreed, if worst came to worst, to stand back to back and fight them off.

This may seem overdrawn to many of our readers of to-day; but if they have ever seen the remains of men and women hacked and mutilated,

as the writer has, and realize as fully as the occupants of the little wagon did that such a fate
awaited them in the event of capture, they too
would have courted death sudden, certain, and
immediate, in preference to that other, more remote but just as sure, and far more terrible.

During the discussion of the situation by Booth
and Hallowell, the speed of the mules had slackened but little; the arm of the latter still plied
that effective lash, and they drew perceptibly
nearer the camp, where there were men enough
to rescue them if they could only be made aware
of their situation; and as they caught the first
glimpse of the tents of the officers and dugouts
of the men, hope sprang up within them, and
life, hanging as it were by a slender cord, seemed
more precious than ever. In the hope of arous-
ing and attracting the attention of some of the
soldiers, they again commenced yelling at the
top of their voices; the mules were panting like
hounds on the chase; wherever the harness
touched them it was white with lather, and
they could not keep on their feet much longer.

Would they hold out until the bridge was
reached, provided they escaped the spears of
the Indians? The whipping and kicking had
little effect on them now; they still continued

in their gallop, but it was slower and more la-
bored than before, and as the Indians fell back
to make fresh charges, the mules also slackened
their gait, and it became almost impossible to
accelerate their motion.

Hallowell kept his whip going mechanically,
and Booth continued his attention to the little
near mule with his foot; but the worn-out animals began to evince unmistakable signs of breaking down, and longing eyes were turned toward
the camp, now so near.

Though the Indians who had torn open the
satchels had not come up, and did not seem in-
clined to further continue the fight, there was
still a sufficient number of the fiends pursuing to
make it interesting; but they could not succeed
in spearing the mules, as at each attempt the
plucky animals would jump sideways or forward
and evade the impending blow.

One gigantic fellow followed them with a determination and valor worthy of a better cause,
the others seeming now to have almost abandoned
the idea of capturing either men or animals; but
this persistent warrior was in all probability related to the young "buck" Booth had killed, and
was thirsting for revenge. At any rate, he was
loth to give up the chase, and followed the wagon

to within a few rods of the bridge, long after the other Indians had fallen back entirely. ،

The little log bridge was now reached; their pursuers had all retreated, but the valorous Hallowell kept the mules at the same galloping gait. This bridge was constructed of half-round logs, and of course was extremely rough. The wagon bounded up and down enough to shake the teeth out of one's head, as the mules went flying over the rude structure. Booth cried out to Hallowell, "No need to drive so fast now—the Indians have all left;" but he answered:

"I ain't going to stop until I get across," and down came the whip, on sped the mules, not breaking their gallop until they pulled up in front of Capt. Conkey's tent. Booth could not stand the fearful bounding of the wagon as it rolled across the bridge, so he crawled out behind and walked up to the quarters.

The rattling of the wagon on the bridge was the first intimation the command had of its returning. The sentinel on the post had been walking his beat on the east side of the long stockade stable to keep out of the cold northwest wind, and had heard nothing of the yelling and talking until they struck the bridge, when he came around the stable, saw the wagon and two or three of the Indians behind, fired his carbine, and thus aroused the camp.

The officers came running out of their tents, the men poured out of their dugouts like a lot of ants, and the wagon and its occupants were soon surrounded by their friends. Capt. Conkey ordered the bugler to sound "boots and saddles," and in less than ten minutes ninety troopers were. mounted, and, with the Captain at their head, started after the Indians.

Lieut. Hallowell reached the line of officers' tents before Booth, and as the latter came up was attempting to rise so as to get out; but each effort only resulted in his falling back. It was thought at first his wounds were the cause, but when asked, "What's the matter? Can't you get out?" replied, "I don't know. I seem to get up only so far." Some one stepped around to the other side to assist him, when it was discovered that the skirt of his overcoat had worked outside the wagon-sheet and hung over the edge, and that three or four of the arrows fired by the Indians had struck the side of the wagon, and passing through the flap of his coat, had pinned him down. Booth pulled the arrows out and helped him up. He was pretty stiff from sitting in his cramped position so long, and his right arm dropped to his side as if struck with paralysis.

While Hallowell walked into Capt. Conkey's tent, assisted by the adjutant and quartermaster, some of the soldiers unhitched the poor mules and led them to the corral. On examining the inside of the wagon, twenty-two arrows were found lying in the bottom, innumerable holes through the sheet made by the passage of arrows, besides two from bullets, and the outside of the bed was scarred from one end to the other.

Booth stood looking on while Hallowell's wounds were being dressed, when the adjutant said, "What makes you shrug your shoulders so, Captain?" Booth replied that he "did not know; something caused it to smart." The adjutant looked, and said, "Well, I should think it *would* smart!—here is an arrow-head sticking into it;" and he tried to pull it out, but it would not come. Capt. Goldsborough then attempted it, but was no more successful than the adjutant. The doctor told them to let it alone and he would take care of it after he had finished with Hallowell, which he soon did, and with his lance cut it out. The point of the arrow had struck the thick part of the shoulder-blade and made two complete turns, wrapping around the muscles, which had to be cut apart before it could be withdrawn.

Both of the principals in the terrible ride were soon attended to and made as comfortable as possible. Booth was not seriously hurt. Hallowell, however, had received two severe wounds: the arrow that had struck in his back penetrated almost to his kidneys, and the wound in his thumb was very painful, caused not so much by the simple contact of the arrow, as the tearing away of the muscles by the shaft while he was whipping the mules; his right arm, too, was swollen fearfully, and became stiff, from the incessant use of it during his drive, and for nearly a month he required help in dressing and undressing. The mules, the veritable saviors of our heroes, were of little account after their memorable trip;—they remained stiff and sore from the rough road and their continued forced speed. Booth and Hallowell went out the next morning to take a look at them as they hobbled around the corral, and from the bottom of their hearts wished them "green fields and pastures new."

About half an hour after the little wagon had returned to Capt. Conkey's camp, a portion of the escort which had been sent out in advance in the morning came galloping up, and from them the following was learned in relation to their movements:

They had started early, as ordered the night before, and moved out on a brisk walk toward Fort Larned. There were plenty of buffalo on the north side of the trail, and they saw no signs of Indians except the absence of buffalo near the river. They kept looking back, and slackened their gait somewhat after getting out four or five miles, to enable the wagon to catch up; and after they had proceeded about a mile beyond the point where the Indians made their first attack, and the wagon had been turned toward the camp, one of the lieutenants said to the other that they were getting too far ahead of the Captain, and suggested the propriety of halting; but Van Antwerp, who was in command, thought it better to leave a part of the company at that spot to wait. Accordingly, a corporal and fifteen men were detailed to remain there until the wagon should arrive, and the remainder moved on toward the fort.

The squad that had been detailed remained beside the trail for half an hour or so, when, becoming chilled, the corporal took them toward the river into a ravine that sheltered both men and horses from the cold northwest wind. There they remained some time, when the corporal, becoming anxious, sent one of the men up the trail to see if the wagon was coming, but he soon returned, reporting nothing in sight. Waiting a few minutes longer, he sent out another man, who on returning reported that the wagon was coming, and had an escort. This last man had seen them a long way off while the Indians were chasing them, and supposed they were an escorting party—which was correct in one sense, but not as he thought and reported.

Remaining in the ravine until the corporal supposed the wagon had arrived nearly opposite, he moved out his squad on the trail, but seeing no wagon, and suspecting something had happened, started his party toward the camp on Walnut creek. They had proceeded but a short distance when one of his men cried out, "Here's an arrow!" Hardly were the words out of his mouth before a second said, "Here's another!" They knew now the reason why the wagon had not come up, and the corporal gave the command to gallop, and away they flew toward the camp. As they successively passed by the empty valises and the innumerable arrows on the trail, they fully realized what kind of an escort had accompanied the little wagon when the soldier had reported, "They are coming, and have an escort."

Capt. Conkey's command returned about midnight. He had seen but one Indian during the entire ride, and he was on the south side of the river, in the sand-hills.

THE TRAGEDY AT TWIN MOUNDS.

An Incident of the Indian War of 1866–'67.

SUSIE RÉAUME.

THE highest points of the divide separating the beautiful valley of the Saline from the Elkhorn, in central Kansas, are two relatively elevated peaks, close together, known all over the region as the Twin Mounds. They can be seen from anywhere within a radius of thirty miles, cutting the deep blue of the sky on clear days as sharply as a summer thundercloud. In their contour they are so exactly similar, even to two white patches of limestone on their southwestern slopes, that their name would immediately suggest itself to a stranger, for never were twins born so perfect in resemblance as these dual masses of disrupted rock.

Under their conical shadow runs the trail of the Mormon hegira to far-off Deseret, when that sect was driven out of Illinois; and also that of General John C. Frémont, on his memorable "Exploring Expedition" across the continent in 1843. Until very recently, when it was ruthlessly cut down, there stood in the valley, on the bank of the Elkhorn, immediately below the mounds, a large oak tree, at the foot of which the General caused that mutineer to be shot, the circumstances of which are related in his itinerary of that wonderful march.

But that was nearly a quarter of a century before the occurrence of the events to be related in this story; and they date back nearly the same length of time from the present. Both trails may still be seen in places where the land has not yet been subordinated to the plow; almost obliterated wagon-tracks in the short buffalo-grass covering that portion of the prairie through which the expedition passed, which each recurring season grow dimmer, and in a few more years will have vanished forever.

—7

The valleys of the Elkhorn and the Saline were heavily timbered — are to-day, relatively. They were a favorite haunt of the Indians; and elk, buffalo, bear, and an occasional panther sought the rocky and vine-involved recesses of the primitive forest.

But the savage and the beasts of the plain have passed away. Now the land is full of harvests and green meads. Yet the Indian summer now as then wraps the hills in its mellow tints; the grass grows brown and rusty as each autumn fills its measure, and the days, as in the long-ago, are as grand as the golden sunshine of that incomparable season of the Great Plains ever lighted up; the mirage, as of old, weaves its fantastic forms out of the charming landscape, and under certain atmospheric conditions a man on top of one of the Twin Mounds will appear, as does the specter of the Brocken, like a huge giant in mid-air.

When Fort Harker, on the Smoky Hill, about fifteen miles south of the Twin Mounds, was established as a military post by Gen. Hancock in the fall of 1866, the whole vast area of central Kansas was the hunting-ground of the cruel and bloodthirsty Cheyennes, Arapahoes, and Kiowas. Their opposition to the intrusion of the whites manifested itself at every opportunity where it

was possible to murder or carry into captivity.
The empire of the plow had just then dawned,
and the march of the homesteader but fairly begun. The satanic genius of Indian hatred brooded
over the beautiful landscape, and the harvest of
the unlabored fields was blood.

It is true a few hardy trappers had for years
roamed over the prairies and camped temporarily
on the banks of the wooded streams, but there was
no attempt at permanent settlement except in
the immediate vicinity of the several forts; but
they were established only from time to time at
remote distances from each other, generally on
the line of the Oregon and Santa Fé trail, under
the protection of which it was alone safe to remain in the country.

About the time the site for the new post of
Fort Harker had been determined upon, and
troops — the Fifteenth Infantry and Gen. Custer's
Seventh Cavalry—were camped on the grassy bottoms of the river and creeks in the vicinity, waiting for their permanent quarters to be erected, a
bold and persistent frontiersman named Paul
Réaume, who had been a pioneer in the wilds of
Wisconsin twenty years before, emigrated from
that State to Kansas.

After looking around for some time, visiting all

the inviting localities of the new commonwealth,
in decided opposition to the advice of the military
authorities at Fort Harker and the commanding
general of the department he took up a "claim"
and established a ranch at a magnificent spring a
few hundred rods north of the base of the Twin
Mounds.

Réaume was a widower, but his eldest daughter,
Susie — dark-haired, rather handsome, and withal
a modest, gentle girl of eighteen — kept house and
acted the rôle of mother to her four young sisters
and brothers, who loved and obeyed her with all
the intensity of their warm natures, (Réaume was
French but one generation removed,) which she
reciprocated in an equal degree. They were a
charming little family, of more means and greater
refinement than are usually found in the average
pioneer immigrant.

The fertile valley stretching many miles north
and south afforded a rich pasturage, and the relatively deep woods on the margin of the Elkhorn a
splendid shelter in winter for the herd of cattle
that Réaume had driven from his old home. So
he built as his needs required a comfortable log
house and spacious corrals, where with an abundance of game all around him, from the trim-
feathered quail to the huge shaggy-coated buffalo,
he settled down to a life of rude contentment.

Of the many Government scouts at Fort Harker, among whom were William F. Cody ("Buffalo Bill"), William Hickok ("Wild Bill") and others, was Jack Hart. Hart was a young light-haired boy, not more than twenty-three years old. He was fairly well educated, neither slangy nor dialectic in expression of thought; courageous as a lion, and endowed with a degree of endurance

SITTING BULL, CROW EAGLE, BUFFALO BILL.

under hardships incident to his vocation that was marvelous in its contemplation by a novice. Jack was a remarkably fine shot with either rifle or revolver. He could toss up an empty oyster can and put every ball out of his two Colts into it before it fell to the ground, and either "crease" or center the heart of an antelope at five hundred yards, as he might elect.

He was as keen on the trail as any Indian, whose original astuteness and strategy he had mastered, and was the superior of the savage, as is any white man when once thoroughly familiar with their cunning. Besides, in that quick perception and determination so essential to success in the moment of danger, when dealing with the wily nomad of the Plains, Hart was unequaled by any other scout I ever knew, and I have intimately known all who have figured at all conspicuously during the past thirty-five years.

Jack was a great favorite with all the officers at the military posts in the whole Department of the Missouri; had their entire confidence, and when any duty in his line became necessary requiring exceptional bravery, judgment and promptness in its execution, Hart was invariably detailed, if present, to perform it.

One day in April, 1867, as he was returning from the Platte river to Fort Harker with a company of the Fifth Calvary he was guiding to the post, they halted at the spring where Réaume had established his ranch, to feed the horses, rest and water. Then for the first time in his life Jack saw Susie Réaume, who was cheerfully preparing an excellent dinner in her father's modest cabin for the officers of the command, who had politely requested of her something to eat.

It was the same old story of mutual love, the
moment their eyes met; and ever after that memorable noon halt, when Hart had a day off he
would mount his own roan broncho Tatonka, ride
across the country to the Twin Mounds, and pour
out his heart's thoughts to the gentle and confiding Susie, who before a month. had elapsed
promised to be his wife.

"There's no chaplain at the post now," said
he, one evening after they were engaged, as they
were sitting on the porch of her father's cabin in
the bright moonlight, discussing plans for the
future and building those airy castles in space as
lovers are wont; "but I heard from the adjutant
yesterday that one had been ordered to Harker
from Fort Leavenworth, under an escort of a
squadron of the Fifth Cavalry. They will be up
in a couple of weeks, and when he arrives we will
get married immediately. Eh! darling?" pleadingly continued Jack.

Susie blushingly assented to Hart's importunity,
and then he told her that he had saved enough to
stock a ranch and build a house; that he proposed
to leave the Government employ as soon as they
were married, take up a "claim" on the Elkhorn
near her father's, so that he would not be separated from her at all, or she from her family. Then

Jack, after cautioning Réaume, who had long before given his consent to the proposed match, to
keep a sharp lookout for Indians, started about
midnight on his lonely ride back to Fort Harker,
where he was obliged to be early the next morning.

SA-TAN-TA.

Jack arrived at the
post long before day-
light, and went to
bed. When he re-
ported to the com-
manding officer the
next morning imme-
diately after guard-
mount, he found
himself (much to
his disgust, now that
he was in love) or-
dered to guide a
scouting-party com-
posed of four companies of the Seventh Cavalry,
commanded by Col. Keogh, to the region of Pawnee Rock and the Great Bend of the Arkansas,
seventy miles to the southwest of Harker, where
the Kiowas, under the leadership of the dreaded
Chief Sa-tan-ta, had been for the past fortnight
successfully raiding the overland coaches and
the freight caravans to New Mexico.

The command to which Hart was attached remained away, having occasional brushes with the Indians, for several weeks. During its absence the allied tribes had become excessively impudent and threatening. They culminated their atrocities in a most fiendish and cruel massacre of the settlers on Spillman creek, upon the receipt of the news of which the Government determined to inaugurate an extended campaign against them, in which Gen. Sheridan was to take the field in person, with such famous Indian-fighters for his lieutenants as Gens. Sully, Custer, Carr, and others. Consequently all the scouting-parties were called in to their respective stations by courier, to prepare for the impending great conflict.

Of course, the moment Hart returned to Fort Harker he made preparations to leave for the ranch at Twin Mounds and the girl who had so photographed herself on the tablets of his memory. It was early the next morning after his arrival at the post; he had shaved, put on a new suit purchased from the sutler, and otherwise made himself presentable after his long scout. But he had hardly cinched the saddle on Tatonka before an orderly came to the corral and informed him that the commanding officer desired his presence at once. So Jack, with terribly depressed feelings and mentally cursing his luck, mounted his horse and rode slowly up to headquarters, where he found the General standing on the porch waiting to receive him.

"Jack," said he, as the scout dismounted, "I'm awfully sorry to be compelled to call upon you to make another trip right away, when you have just returned from such a long one, but the fact is there's not another scout at the post; they are all away. I want you to start immediately for the Saline. Part of the Fifth Cavalry are *en route* from Fort Saunders here, and will probably reach the ford northwest of Fort Hays sometime to-day. It is now only six o'clock," looking at his watch; "you can reach there as soon as they do — before, if you start now. So go at once and guide them in. They don't know anything about that country on the river. You remember how terribly broken it is out there. Here are some dispatches you are to give to whomever you find in command;" and he handed the scout a small package of papers.

"All right, sir," replied Hart, as he put the bundle in the breast-pocket of his flannel shirt; "I'm off now, as soon as I go to my quarters for my saddlebags and carbine."

With a sad heart as he cast his eyes on the blue

cones of the Twin Mounds, looming up so suggest-
ively of the ranch at their base, Jack left the
post in a few minutes after his interview with
Gen. Sully, fully mindful of the responsible duty
intrusted to him. Hart made excellent time. He
was anxious to get back as soon as possible. By
two o'clock he had crossed the Saline, and when
about three miles the other side of where the
handsome little village of Sylvan to-day nestles
so picturesquely in the wealth of woods surrounding, he met the troops, to whose commander he
reported, and delivered his dispatches. He turned
with them to the river, where, as it was now past
three, the command went into camp for the night.

After grazing Tatonka for half an hour, feeding
him some corn, and eating his own dinner, the
thought suddenly struck Jack to ask permission
to go over to the ranch at the foot of the Twin
Mounds, whose dual peaks were plainly visible
only fifteen miles away to the southeast as the
crow flies. The colonel cordially granted Jack's
request. He promised to join the column on the
trail early in the morning before it had marched
any great distance; then, at the commanding
officer's suggestion, Jack drew in the sand with
his finger a rough map of the route to Fort
Harker, supplementing it by pointing out certain

divides and ledges of rock that could plainly be seen on the trail from where the colonel and the scout stood.

When Jack had finished he left the camp for the spot where he had given his heart more than two months before, his soul filled with rapture at the prospect of soon meeting again the gentle girl he loved.

His horse was a medium-sized broncho, full of power and endurance, which he knew could easily make Réaume's ranch in three hours. That would bring him there about seven o'clock, in time for supper, and more than an hour and a half before dark. So he struck a bee-line for the Mounds, his feelings better imagined than described; an ecstasy indefinable except to those whose experience has been similar to that of the overhappy scout.

The sun was just sinking below the horizon when Jack arrived at the Elkhorn, in the immediate vicinity of the ranch. A flood of golden light poured into the beautiful little valley as he crossed the ford and entered the circular grove, in the middle of which Réaume had built his log cabin and corrals. As he rode toward the place where the cluster of rude huts should be, his eyes, which were ordinarily as keen and as bright as an

eagle's, suddenly filled, for he looked upon a scene
that caused his bronzed cheeks to blanch and an
exclamation of horror to escape his lips. The
cabin was roofless, and the green timber compos-
ing its sides and ends was still slowly burning.

"Cheyennes!" he muttered with set teeth, as
he unslung his carbine, spurred his horse forward,
while a prayer for the safety of the girl he loved
was formulated in his brain. When he reached
the opening where the once happy home was so
picturesquely located he drew up on the reins, and
as Tatonka stopped a deep groan escaped Jack.
Lying under the mighty trees, close to the ruins
of the cabin, were the scalped and mutilated remains of Réaume and his four youngest children.

But where was Susie, the woman he loved?
Dazed and stupefied for a moment, Jack began
to search for her body. She was not with the rest
of the murdered family. "Oh, my God!" he
cried in his agony, "has she been saved for a fate
worse than death! Carried off a miserable captive
among the soulless savages? Great God, no! I
cannot think of it. Sooner would I see her here
dead with the others!"

Although almost overcome with grief, and furious with passion as these thoughts, so terrible
in their contemplation, crowded thick upon his

brain, he was determined not to lose his self-control. Pausing for a moment, cautiously looking around to assure himself that none of the paint-bedaubed fiends were lurking in the timber, he dismounted, tied his horse to an oak sapling, walked to where his dead friends lay, and silently contemplated the horrid butchery. He dared not think of the probable fate of the faithful young girl who had promised to be his wife, but he uttered bitter curses against the demons who had so wantonly, and without the slightest provocation, annihilated the peaceful little family. He swore to himself that he would have ten lives for one, in his determined revenge. He turned away, sick at heart, from these victims of Indian hatred, and walked slowly toward the spring to quench his feverish thirst and to collect his dazed ideas.

It was six or seven rods from where the cabin had stood to the wall of rock in the hillside out of which the water gushed, and it was completely hidden by a dense growth of cottonwoods, willows and elders, covering more than an acre. As he approached the edge of this tangled thicket, a low moan reached his ear; whether animal or human, so faint was it, he could not distinguish.

Stopping for an instant, every sense on the alert, he cocked his carbine, and listened atten-

tively.   The strange sound was repeated.   He
moved cautiously on the narrow trail.   Then suddenly as he arrived at the spring, which made
quite a pool as it fell from a shelf of sandstone,
with a cry of horror from his lips he saw prone
on the ground, her pale mouth just touching the
water's edge as it flowed in a diminutive rivulet,
the apparently lifeless body of Susie Réaume.

" Susie, my darling ! " cried he, as he knelt rev-
erently by her side and kissed her forehead, for he
believed her certainly dead.   But the girl's eyes
opened as she felt the warm impress of his lips,
and she looked up into his anxious face with an
unmistakable glance of recognition, vainly essay-
ing to speak.

" Oh, Susie, are you seriously hurt ?   Tell me,
if you can," he lovingly pleaded, as he then for
the first time noticed, with fear depicted on his
countenance, a pool of dried blood on the sod beneath her.

After an evident struggle she laboredly gasped :
" Yes — Jack — here," touching her right side
with her left hand, causing her much effort to
accomplish it.

Jack at once commenced to unfasten her dress,
but she instinctively attempted to raise her arms
to prevent him, while a delicate blush spread over
her pale face.

"Susie, dear," said Jack, as he understood what her motion was intended to convey to him, "there are no woman's hands here to do what under the circumstances must be done; so, darling, let there be no false modesty. I want to save you, and you want to live."

Upon this appeal she made no more resistance, but her eyes closed, and the glow of her maiden delicacy deepened, while Jack, with the most sacred feelings, cut open her bodice with his sheath-knife and exposed her virgin bosom to the evening breeze. On the right side, immediately on a line with her shoulder, he discovered an ugly lance-wound, which had bled so profusely that she had fainted, and was almost exhausted when Jack found her. The wound had evidently stopped flowing some time since, and fortunately the blade had not penetrated her lungs; at least so thought Jack in his careful and gentle examination, determining the matter from the fact that there was no hemorrhage from her mouth, and he silently thanked God.

It was now long after sundown. In the lingering twilight he carefully washed the wound with water, using a portion of her skirt he had cut off for the purpose. Completing this office, and binding on a wet compress, Jack then moved her tenderly to a mat of soft buffalo-grass near by, made a pillow of his saddle, and a covering for her out of his saddle blanket, then busied himself in making her a cup of coffee, a supply of which and a small pot he always carried with him.

The coffee and some hardtack he had, revived the wounded girl very materially, reduced the incipient fever which had set in, and permitted her to fall into a gentle slumber; while Jack, under the brilliant constellations of the incomparable June night, nursed her through its silent watches. The poor fellow leaned patiently over her with looks of the most tender solicitude, bathing her temples now and then with water from the spring when she became the least restless, and occasionally running his fingers through her dark ringlets with the fondness of a young but constantly growing affection—for it was his first love, and he had given his soul up to it with all the strength and weakness of his passion.

The sun, though not yet above the horizon of the valley, was just gilding the crests of the Twin Mounds next morning when Susie awoke with a glance of approving affection on Jack. Although she did not speak, there is a language of looks which is sufficient for the purposes of love. As

—8

he quietly kissed her he understood it perfectly, and it filled his soul with joy.

Jack then, after his ablutions at the spring, made a little fire, put on his coffee-pot, which soon boiled, and while it was settling he tenderly washed the wounded girl's face and placed a fresh compress on the cruel hole in her side.

After Susie had partaken of her frugal breakfast, she was able to converse a few minutes. She expressed herself in words that were music in Jack's ears, of the deepest gratitude and love for the care he had bestowed upon her, assuring him that but for his opportune coming and devotion, she would hours since have been dead.

"Do you think, Susie, you could ride on my horse?" pleadingly inquired Jack. "We could reach Fort Harker early in the afternoon, if you have strength enough to sit in the saddle, and can bear the fatigue. I am certain you need a doctor's care and a woman's nursing. Were it possible to leave you here, I would make the post in three hours, and bring back an ambulance for you. But that would require every minute from now until four o'clock; and to compel you to remain here and alone until I return, with the Indians perhaps hovering around, cannot be thought of."

Susie was now sitting up, leaning against the trunk of a big elm to which Jack had carried her, in order that she might be more comfortable; and in answer she said:

"I think I am strong enough, Jack. I *must* be. That is the only thing that can be done. I have n't much fever now, and my wound has n't bled any since yesterday. Let 's try, at least. I 've lots of courage—you know that—and I believe that I can make the trip."

Jack then watered Tatonka, saddled him, and after tying him to a tree, told Susie he would go up on the hill and make a reconnoissance before they started; that he would be gone only about ten or fifteen minutes, and not to worry during his absence. .

The sun was fairly above the horizon when Jack, with only his sheath-knife, started for the bluffs above the creek bottom, where he could see over the country for miles. He wanted to satisfy himself whether there were any Indians skulking in the vicinity, as he dared not take such desperate chances, handicapped with the helpless girl, as he would if he were going to make the trip to Fort Harker alone.

He had not forgotten his promise of the afternoon before, to join the cavalry column and guide it to the post; consequently he was somewhat disturbed at first. But when he left the colonel he of course never imagined that such a fate had befallen Réaume's ranch and the girl Jack loved. So the scout did not, when he considered the matter a moment, weigh his duty in the scales of his affection. He would have sacrificed place, friends and everything to save his affianced. What man would blame him ?

He had just reached the second bottom above the creek and was emerging from the heavy growth of timber out on the prairie at the foot of the most southerly of the Twin Mounds, when he was confronted by a monstrous she-panther, with three young ones not more than six weeks old. Ordinarily, that animal of the *genus felis* will not attack man,—preferring, rather, to shrink from his presence, unless provoked by wounds. But in this instance both Hart and the panther were face to face on the edge of the woods before they were aware of the fact. Which was the more surprised, the man or the beast, it would have been difficult to determine.

If there had been no little ones with her, in all probability the panther would have incontinently bounded into the timber at the first glance of Jack's eyes; but the presence of the kittens aroused the maternal instinct for their safety. So, with a low growl and a characteristic "spit" at him, she flew at the scout's breast, fastening her great claws into his shoulders before he could draw his knife, and they both fell by the sheer impetus of the cat's onset.

Jack, unfortunately for himself at this juncture, had left his carbine and revolvers with Susie. She could use them very effectually in case of emergency, but she was too far away to be able to hear him if he should call, and too weak to come if she could hear him. Now, his only dependence for defense from the murderous attack of the ferocious beast was his knife, but he was an expert in its use.

They struggled fearfully, the infuriated animal endeavoring to insert its teeth in the scout's throat, which luckily he succeeded in preventing by the dexterous use of his knife. But in the awfully unequal battle he was terribly cut by the sharp, active claws of the enraged beast, and was bleeding profusely from more than a dozen wounds already inflicted on his shoulders, legs and body. He had, fortunately, been able to keep the cat's great paws off his face.

At last, by one desperate effort Jack succeeded in giving a home thrust in the region of the crea-

ture's heart, which ended the struggle; luckily
for him, too, for at that moment he swooned from
loss of blood.   The panther loosened her hold—
she was dead.

This final effort of the scout occurred on the
extreme edge of a rocky shelf, whither both man
and beast had been forced during their desperate
fight.   Below this shelf, at a distance of only a
few feet, fortunately, the level prairie hugged
the timber, the latter throwing a deep shade
over the spot.   Into this grassy little place both
Hart and the panther fell—he insensible from
loss of blood, with the lifeless beast alongside
him.

In the cavalry camp on the Saline the troopers
were busily grooming their horses at the picket-
line.   The captains of companies near by were
superintending this important duty, while the
colonel, surrounded by a group of officers, nearly
all of whom were smoking their matutinal pipes,
stood in front of headquarters tent, drinking in
the charming landscape and delicious freshness
of the early summer morning.   Suddenly, as his
eyes happened to rest upon the double cones of
the Twin Mounds that loomed up blue and clearly
defined in the coming light from the east, he

pointed in their direction with a field-glass he
had in his hand, and exclaimed:

"Look, gentlemen, look! A mirage! a mirage!"

Every one turned; and presently, while all were
gazing with enchantment on the strange phenom-
enon, far above the peaks, in the sky, but inverted,
two moving figures appeared, surrounded by that
waving purple mist characteristic of the mirage

THE MIRAGE.

on the Great Plains. One of the celestial appari-
tions was in the similitude of a man, the other of
a beast. Both were gigantic and exaggerated in
outline; both were grappling in a deadly struggle!

Every soldier stopped his work to watch the
curious picture suspended in the heavens; some
regarded it with a superstitious awe, thoroughly
frightened at the manifestation, which they never
dreamed of as within the range of possibilities.

The colonel recognized the huge figure of the man in the clouds, disproportioned as he was, to be the scout who had left him the afternoon before, but what the beast was none of the men could make out.

"Great Cæsar!" cried the colonel; "what a place for a battle, away up there in the clouds! It reminds me of Lookout Mountain, when I was with Hooker."

Every one intently watched the strange combat, filled with excitement at the novelty of the thing, until presently the figures appeared to fall over an immense precipice and vanish, although they seemed to disappear with an upward movement. Then there was nothing left but the inverted mounds, the woods and the prairie of the wonderful mirage; it, too, was all dispelled in a few moments more.

The colonel turned to his adjutant and ordered "boots and saddles" sounded at once.

"For we must be off," said he, addressing the officers around him generally. "Life may depend upon our promptness in reaching the scene of that strange conflict."

In less than a quarter of an hour the column had moved out, headed in a "bee-line" for the Twin Mounds, every man in the whole command

as anxious as his comrade to reach the place, for
all were excited over what they had witnessed.

It required four hours of brisk marching before
they arrived on the plateau at the base of the
Mounds, and by that time it was past eleven
o'clock, and intensely hot. The command halted
there, while the colonel, the adjutant, the surgeon, several other officers and a detail of five
enlisted men instituted a search for the missing
scout.

In a little while they found the bodies of Hart
and the panther close together, lying in the shade
of the huge oaks, where they had fallen in their
last struggle, and when they had disappeared to
those who had watched the combat from their
camp on the Saline.

Upon examination, the surgeon discovered that
the scout was alive, but terribly lacerated by the
sharp claws and teeth of the panther, as well as
badly bruised in consequence of his fall from the
ledge of rocks, though no bones were broken, nor
were any of his wounds necessarily serious. He
had merely become insensible from loss of blood
and exhaustion incident to the awful struggle.
The doctor placed a flask of brandy to the unconscious man's mouth, which he pried open with
Jack's own knife, still clutched in his right hand

when discovered; and in a few moments, as the stimulating liquor reached his stomach, he slowly opened his eyes, looked around in a bewildered manner at first, then apparently taking in the situation of affairs at a glance, partially raised himself, and in a hoarse whisper, pointing in the direction where he had left her, said:

"Susie Réaume! Near the spring! Quick, for God's sake!"

"Who?" replied the astonished doctor; "Susie, a woman, here too?"

Jack had by this time gotten over his dizziness somewhat, and was able feebly though intelligently to convey the story of the awful massacre at the ranch, his relations to the wounded girl, and the state of affairs when attacked by the panther. Then looking at the sun, and realizing that hours must have elapsed since he had left Susie, he urged the doctor to go at once, upon which he attempted to get on his feet to guide him to the spot, but he was too weak yet, and would have fallen if one of the men had not caught him.

"No! no!" exclaimed the doctor, when he divined Jack's intention; "don't try to walk yet. I'll leave one of the troopers to look after you and I'll go and attend to the young girl immediately. You 'll be all right in half an hour; then you can follow."

So, with directions from Jack, the doctor, the colonel and two soldiers started for the spring, which they found without any difficulty, the trail to that point having been explained in such a clear manner by the anxious scout.

Entering the maze of willows by a well-beaten trail that led from the kitchen door of the destroyed cabin, they found Susie in nearly the same position in which Jack had left her early in the morning, sitting on the grass against the big elm, weak and feverish. She involuntarily gave a little cry of surprise when she saw the officers approaching, and with a slight blush mantling her cheeks, laid the rifle she had raised from the ground at her side when she first heard footsteps, back in its place, and bowed her head gracefully in response to the colonel's courteous salutation. Both he and the doctor were surprised to find so much refinement and culture as Susie evinced, in such an unlooked-for place.

"Miss Susie," said the colonel, as he irresistibly lifted his hat to the charming picture of rusticity, "I have brought our surgeon, at Jack's request, who will see what he can do for you, and then we 'll find means to transport you comfortably to Fort Harker, where you can be properly cared for. The doctor will tell you all about Jack's mishap—there, don't be alarmed," as Susie made a convulsive start; "he's all right, and will be here presently." Then bowing again, the colonel and his two men retired some distance, while the doctor, as modestly as possible, examined the gentle girl's wounds, and told her the story of Jack's strange adventure.

Susie Réaume was a girl of the strongest affections, but not in the least degree demonstrative. Her grief at the horrible fate of her father, brothers and sisters was as deep as the circumstances were appalling, her love for the young scout as pure as it would be enduring; but on both subjects of the sorrow which had come to her in a single day she was reticent, or communicated so little that the first impressions of the colonel and the doctor were that she was as emotionless as a marble statue. There was never a greater error of judgment: concealment of her anguish was a prominent characteristic of her nature, while she suffered unutterable mental torture.

By the time the doctor had finished dressing Susie's wounds the command was well established in camp on the stream, and dinner in progress. Jack had returned to the spring too, holding a conference with the colonel as soon as he arrived there, explaining that he was not a quarter of a mile away from a good trail to Fort Harker, that ran a little distance west of the Elkhorn, where they now were.

Jack was thinking and congratulating himself upon the curious chain of circumstances which had thwarted all his plans, provided better for the wounded Susie, and at the same time saved his honor, if indeed it were at all involved, in breaking his word to the colonel.

Both of the doctor's patients in a short time received some excellent nourishment, prepared by the hospital steward out of the medical stores, under the surgeon's direction, reviving the wounded girl materially and putting Jack fairly "on his feet" again, for he was "as tough as a knot."

About half-past two the column was ready to move out. Susie was made comfortable on a litter, fashioned after the Indian method of transporting their wounded, constructed of saplings and blankets, which was carefully slung between two pack-mules of the supply train, respectively led by two troopers detailed for that duty. This novel equipage the colonel ordered to march in advance of the column, so that the dust raised by the company's horses should not annoy Susie;

while Jack, who was able to mount Tatonka, though he was terribly sore and stiff, rode alongside of her and piloted the command on the trail. Before they left the ruined ranch, however, the colonel caused the bodies of the unfortunate Réaumes to be temporarily interred and large stones put over their graves, to prevent the wolves from digging up and eating the flesh off their bones, as it was Hart's intention to have them taken to the post and decently buried in the little cemetery there.

After an eventful march the command arrived at Fort Harker just as the sun was setting, where Susie was kindly cared for, and Jack went to his own quarters, to be patched up and plastered by the post surgeon.

Hart was out and ready for duty inside of a week; but Susie did not gain rapidly. She seemed to be slowly wasting away with a fever, though the wound in her side had closed, and there was no longer danger from that source. It was the terrible agony of her soul; she did not complain, and the doctor was puzzled. The awful mental strain incident to what she had passed through, coupled with the morbid fear that the marriage with the man she loved could not be consummated, was doing its work. Only time, the great

healer of sorrows, could bring relief, and both she
and Jack were impatient.

The weeks dragged their weary length along,
and the golden October days came before she was
convalescent; but with that subdivision of the
year came also the inauguration of that celebrated
winter campaign against the allied tribes, for
which Gen. Sheridan had been making vigorous
preparations all summer. Of course there could
be no marriage now until the war was over, and it
lasted (officially) for one hundred and sixty-three
days, counting from the 21st of October, but virtually ending with Gen. Custer's annihilation of
Black Kettle and his band of warriors in the
battle of the Washita, in November.

At last, in May, 1869, that month of floral
beauty on the Central Plains, on a delicious Sab-
bath morning, Jack and Susie were married by
the post chaplain in the large unoccupied ward of
the hospital at Fort Harker, which had been gar-
landed with wild flowers, roses predominating, and
great bunches of the creamy-petaled yucca, for the
occasion.

Gens. Sheridan, Custer, Sully, and all the officers, with their wives, who were part of the garrison stationed there, graced the ceremony with
their presence. Buffalo Bill, Wild Bill, and all

the other famous scouts on duty at Fort Harker,
were also present; and many substantial presents
were received from all the distinguished guests by
the favored couple.

Nearly a quarter of a century has elapsed since
then. All the famous generals mentioned are
dead. Hart is now a prosperous ranchman, with
large herds of mild-eyed Jerseys and broad-backed
Shorthorns peacefully grazing in his extensive pastures. On the porch of his beautiful home, Susie,
now a stately matron, and Jack with his pipe in
his mouth, may be seen sitting in their large arm-
chairs at the close of day, resting from the labors
the ranch imposes. A bevy of handsome children
are busy with hammock or swing under the great
trees of the lawn; and as the twilight gathers,
the old folks relate to the little ones the story of
those terrible hours on the Elkhorn so many years
ago—a picture on "memory's walls" that time
can never efface.

WAL. HENDERSON.

IN one of the busy little mining camps just over the range in New Mexico there prowled around, about twenty-five years ago, a notorious character whose life was made up of desperate adventures, and whose tragic death, which is the subject of this sketch, illustrates the inevitable fate of the average border bully.

Wal. Henderson was born and "raised"—as he termed it—in Missouri. He came over the mountains into the New Mexico mines from Colorado soon after the first discovery of gold in the Moreno hills, where he staked off a claim in Humbug Gulch, and commenced working in an apparently honest way. He was a rough, illiterate fellow, possessing the physique of a giant, courageous as a she-grizzly with cubs, and such a dead shot with his revolver that he soon became a terror to the whole mountain population. He was a desperado in its fullest sense, without one redeeming quality, except that he was kind to his dog, a wicked-looking cur, fit companion for such a surly master.

WAL. HENDERSON.

Any more intercourse with Wal. than was absolutely necessary was carefully avoided by every
one, and the idea of getting into a dispute with
him—who would rather shoot than eat—never

entered the heads of those who worked claims in
the vicinity; so that, virtually, he commanded
the respect of a king. One afternoon Wal. was
seized with a desire to start off on a little pros-
pecting tour to another portion of the range,
where he suspected the existence of a quartz lead.
He left his claim in the "Gulch" only partially
opened, never dreaming for an instant that anyone would have the temerity to jump it in his
absence, after they had discovered that he owned
it; which he took good care they could easily
learn, for before he went he asked one of his more
educated neighboring miners to "come over and
cut his name" on a dead pine stump that stood
near the mouth of his pit.

This friend was nothing loth to oblige his surly
comrade, so just after dinner he came over, and
with his keen bowie-knife slashed out a huge

"Wal henDerSoN his KLaime"

on the dead stump.

It took him nearly two hours to complete his
literary labors, while Wal. stood by impatiently
watching him, and when his friend had just finished the last touch of his rude letters, remarked:

"Well, I guess there hain't no one goin' for to
touch that thar."

Then, swinging his pick and shovel over his shoulder, he whistled to his dog, took his bearings by a look at the sun, started down the cañon on a sort of shuffling trot, and was soon out of sight.

He was gone three days. When he returned he found that his ground had been "jumped" by a party of Irish miners who had come into the diggings during his absence.

Wal., in as quiet a manner as his bulldog nature permitted, told them to "git!" But they swore they would hold the claim in spite of him; and if he was as big as "Finn McCool" they would fight him.

Wal. smothered his rage for the moment, coolly walked off to his cabin, where he armed himself with two revolvers, a Spencer carbine, and a wicked-looking IXL blade, and started back to the gulch, determined to drive the intruders away, or kill them if necessary — it mattered little as to choice.

"Git out of this! — quick! — jump! or I'll fill you full o' holes!" was Wal.'s greeting as on his return he came in sight of the intruders. But one of the plucky Irishmen made a break for Wal., intending to finish him by a well-directed blow from his shovel.

Wal. quick as thought brought down his revol-

ver, killing his man instantly, the bullet hitting
him in the forehead directly between the eyes—
a spot that was Wal.'s invariable target, which in
his list of nearly a score of victims he never failed
to center.

The two now thoroughly frightened companions
of the dead miner fled to camp and told the story
of the murder.

Wal., believing that he would have a crowd on
his heels in a little while, started hurriedly for
his cabin, proposing to "light out" for a while
as he said; but a mob of plucky men intercepted
him. He was arrested, taken to camp, and confined in a little log building, around which a
guard was placed.

As the news of Wal.'s latest exploit spread
around the hills, the Irish miners flocked in from
all directions, bent on revenge. The people of
the town expected a general outbreak between the
Irish and American elements, if any resistance was
offered to the infuriated friends of the murdered
man in their attempt to take Wal. from the improvised jail, which they openly proclaimed they
would do as soon as night came on.

The building used for the incarceration of Wal.
was an abandoned log store, about sixteen feet
square; the interstices of the logs were "chinked"

with mud, and the whole surmounted by a brush-
and-dirt roof. In the corner of the room, after
the Mexican fashion, a huge but rude fireplace
had been constructed of stone and earth, from
which a large chimney composed of the same material communicated with the open air through
the roof above.

No sooner had the heavy door closed on Wal.
than he began an accurate survey of his quarters,
with a view of escaping as soon as the mob he
confidently expected should make their appearance.

One glance at the immense fireplace, which
yawned like the opening to a cave, and a look
at the clear sky above through the chimney, satisfied him that he would be out of his prison and
up some mountain gulch before his intended cap-
tors could think twice.

Shortly after dark a motley crowd of rough
miners, half-crazed with the villainous liquors
they had been drinking all the afternoon, assembled at the jail. They at once ordered the guard
away, fired their pistols in the air, and made the
very hills ring with their curses and imprecations
upon the prisoner within the little hut.

Wal. meanwhile had determined to escape; in
fact, at the very time the crowd had reached the

door he was on the roof, quietly waiting for the mob to make a rush inside, at which moment he proposed to leap to the ground from the rear of the building.

He waited for the signal, which soon came in the shape of a volley of pistol- and carbine-shots, and a wild yell from the would-be avengers, who with a desperate rush made for the door. Under the pressure it flew from its fastenings, and swung open with a loud report, throwing half a dozen of the mob upon the dirt floor.

For a moment or two no one could enter, as those nearest the door became wedged together, while the pressure from the crowd in the rear held them more securely imprisoned than Wal., who at this juncture jumped from the roof, and, to use his own expression, "lit out —— lively."

When the crowd became aware that Wal. had escaped they threatened to lynch the guard, and but for the intercession of some of the cooler-headed and less drunken members of the party, no doubt their threats would have been carried into execution.

They divided into little bands and scoured the camp, visiting every suspected house or hole where their game might possibly be secreted, and it was not until early morning that the search was abandoned.

The following day the events of the preceding night were fully discussed, and as many conjectures were suggested in relation to Wal.'s escape and whereabouts as there were groups of men: each had his own theory, each knew exactly how and when he got away.

Old Sam Bartlett, a short, thick-set, grizzly veteran miner, expressed it as his opinion that "Wal. went up that thar chimbly, and by this yer time is well heeled somewhar near camp, surrounded by a battery of small-arms, ready to fight the whole outfit."

Sam's surmises proved true. No sooner had Wal. made his escape than he went to his own den for a moment, to secure arms and ammunition; then to an abandoned tunnel about a mile up the nearest gulch, where he immediately commenced to fortify his position, prepared to sell his life as dearly as possible if the mob pursued him. As he afterward said, "Did not intend to pass in his checks until he had made a sieve of a few of 'em."

The Mexican woman with whom he lived proved a faithful ally. Under the shadow of the night she secretly conveyed food and blankets, never revealing to a soul where her "Americano" was; always earnestly denying any knowledge of the fugitive.

For nearly a week Wal. lived in the abandoned
mining tunnel. At the expiration of that time,
when the excitement had somewhat subsided, and
it was generally supposed he had fled the country,
he quietly walked into camp at midnight, broke
open a stable, took out a horse, saddled him, and
galloped off to Taos, which place he reached next
morning. In justice to Wal., let it be said he·
was not a professional horse-thief — he had not
gotten so low as that; but having perfect faith in
the old saw that "self-preservation is the first law
of nature," he seized upon the only reliable means
to escape strangling by a mob. On his arrival at
Taos, where he felt secure, he returned the animal
to his owner with thanks, complimenting him on
his architectural skill in constructing a stable
that could be entered so easily, and upon the endurance of his horse that had carried him so well.

A little more than a month later, the camp was
somewhat startled one afternoon at seeing Wal.
riding down the main street mounted on a Mexican pony, with four revolvers buckled around his
waist and a carbine slung across his back. Halting in front of a saloon, he alighted, and with a
devil-may-care sort of a nod to the loafers hanging around, invited them all in to take a drink.
To the crowd at the bar he related his adventures

since he had been among them; said he was tired
of Taos, and had come back to look after his mining interests up Humbug Gulch, which he thought
he had neglected too long. He added "if any
gentlemen (?)" were sympathizers with the would-
be stranglers, he would be pleased to step out on
the street and give them an ,exhibition of his
peculiar manner of managing the portable battery
he had provided himself with. No one seeming
particularly anxious to witness the proffered en-
tertainment, war was not declared, and after a
round or two of "Taos lightning," as whisky was
called in those days, Wal. quietly mounted his
horse and made his way toward his little "dug-
out," where he was met by his faithful Señora
and provided with a bountiful repast of tortillas
and frijoles (corn cake and beans).

The excitement in camp gradually exhausted
itself, and it was mutually agreed that Wal. should
not be molested if he kept away from Humbug
Gulch.

Wal. apparently accepted the situation; turned
his attention to the laudable ambition of supplying the camp with cord-wood, and almost any day
thereafter could be seen coming into town with
his load.

One day about two months after he had settled

himself down to legitimate pursuits, while sitting
in a saloon, fatigued by a somewhat arduous
morning's work, a party of Irish miners entered,
all of whom were more or less under the influence
of liquor. After bandying words with Wal. in
reference to his claim and the murder of their
companion, one, rather more bold then discreet,
approached Wal. holding a large stone, and said,
"Be jabers, Wal., you would look better dead
than alive;" when Wal., as quick as thought,
drew his pistol, and drawing a bead on the Irish-
man, said, "Drop that rock!"

The stone dropped. Wal. quietly resumed his
seat without another word, replaced his pistol in
its holster, coolly lighted his pipe, and commenced to smoke. The gang were evidently bent
on mischief; but Wal. could not be intimidated,
and made no move to leave his seat, but kept his
keen eye on every act of the drunken mob.

He listened coolly and indifferently for a while
to their coarse jests and braggadocio threats cast at
him. But there comes a moment when "patience
ceases to be a virtue," and comes soonest to men
of such caliber as Wal. When another of the
belligerents approached too near with an outra-
geous remark, Wal. jumped to his feet and said,
"By ——! I think I'll kill one of you just for

luck, and put a stop to this —— nonsense."
Drawing out his pistol he fired, the ball, as always, taking effect in the bridge of his victim's nose, passing through the right eye and coming out in front of the ear.

At the report of the pistol a crowd rushed in, but no one attempted to interfere with Wal., who took a position against the side of the room, where he invited any one who wanted him, to "step up; but if any one did he would make a sieve of him."

No one desirous of being converted into that useful article just then, not a soul stepped forward.

The alcalde* and sheriff were sent for, and soon arrived. Wal. gave himself up, and was remanded to his old quarters, the little log jail from which he had so successfully made his escape by way of the huge chimney, on a former occasion.

The drunken companions of the murdered miner immediately upon the arrest of Wal. started off to muster up a crowd of their countrymen, determined this time to mete out summary vengeance upon the assassin of their comrade.

To preclude the possibility of an escape on the part of the prisoner, an additional guard was em-

*The Spanish title of a magistrate corresponding to justice of the peace.

ployed to watch the outside of the jail, and two men were posted on the roof—"no goin' up that thar chimbley this time."

Shortly after dark another mob, composed of the friends of Wal.'s last victim, poured into camp from the gulches and hills and proceeded directly to the jail, determined that this. time their game should not slip through their fingers.

In a few moments the infuriated and howling would-be lynchers forced the door of the building open in the same manner as they had done before, but their bird had flown—Wal. was not there!

Knowing the desperate character of the men who had come to take his life, Wal. had resolved to make a determined effort to get away from them if possible, when he first heard them surging and howling in the distance, and putting all his quick wits at work, soon decided what might be done.

Standing at the side of the door as it was crushed from its fastenings, he allowed the crowd to tumble and rush pell-mell into the dark room, while he quickly slipped past them out into the street, walked slowly to the first corner, then shot into the night—and was free!

The rage and disappointment of the exasperated miners on the discovery that their man had again eluded them, can better be imagined than described.

Wal. proceeded to his little home, took one of his horses from the stable, rode rapidly out of camp over a mountain trail, and in a few hours was miles away, where he found a safe retreat.

The disappointed crowd on discovering that for the present at least Wal. was beyond their power, slowly retired to their homes, swearing they would kill Wal. on sight if he ever made his appearance in camp again.

But a few days elapsed before Wal. again dropped into town; though strange as it may seem, no attempt was made to arrest him.

For weeks everything about camp moved along quietly, and it was hoped that further disturbance was at an end. One afternoon, however, while Wal. was standing in front of one of the little stores scattered at intervals through the long main street of the town, engaged in conversation with a lot of miners who had congregated there, a horseman came galloping up the principal thoroughfare, halting directly in front of the door where Wal and his companions were talking.

Taking a single glance at Wal., he exclaimed, "You are the man I am looking for!" and drawing his revolver, commenced shooting. He fired three shots in rapid succession, neither of which, however, took effect; but before he could cock his pistol again, which he was in the act of doing, Wal. had "drawn a bead" on him and fired.

The ball struck him in the trigger thumb and thereby turned, or it would have found its proper center between the eyes. Finding himself disabled, the rider put spurs to his horse and fled to the friendly shelter of the nearest ravine, but soon returned dismounted, as he discovered that he had not been followed by the terrible Wal.

A crowd gathered around to "shoot the wretch who had so deliberately jeopardized the lives of innocent citizens"; but he called out that he was wounded—"for God's sake not to kill him!" He would give himself up quietly if he could be permitted to see a doctor.

The doctor happened to be sitting in front of his office near by, and took him in and amputated his thumb.

He was then turned over to the sheriff, who placed him in an unoccupied log building, and appointed a guard to watch him.

During the night, however, following in the footsteps of the illustrious Wal., he eluded the vigilance of the guard, made good his escape and ran to the mountains, where he was received by friends, who were determined to protect him from rearrest.

The following day word was sent the doctor to come out and dress his wounds. Obeying the summons, the doctor found him within a hundred yards of his cabin, at the side of a mining-ditch, surrounded by an array of pistols, carbines, and knives, determined to resist any attempt to re-arrest him, the point selected commanding every avenue of approach up the mountain-slope.

Here he remained several days. He sent word to the alcalde, through some of his friends, that he would die before giving himself up to the "stranglers," but would submit if soldiers were to come for him.

Upon this message of defiance no further effort was made to capture him, and the town lapsed once more into its wonted quietude. Even Henderson became remarkably docile, no further disturbances occurring between him and the miners — the trouble ending, apparently, by mutual consent.

Some months subsequent to the incidents related in the foregoing, the little camp was again thrown into a state of excitement, in consequence of a report of the robbery of the mail in the cañon between Elizabethtown and Ute creek.

It was bruited about, and proved true, that when the coach (which made tri-weekly trips between the camp and the Cimarron, to connect with the great Southern Overland Line) reached a lonely point in the cañon where the road was narrow and wound around a side-hill covered with a dense growth of scrubby pines, three disguised men would slip out and order the driver to halt; then, without moving from their place on either side of the confined pass, with their rifles pointed toward him, demand that the express box be thrown from the boot.

This modest request was always complied with, after which they ordered the driver to move on, much to the relief of the thoroughly frightened conductor, and the two or three passengers inside.

Five or six depredations of this character were committed in the course of a month. The people in camp began to have their suspicions aroused, and many were the conjectures as to who the guilty parties could be.

A company was formed to scour the cañon, but not even a clue of the highwaymen could be found, nor a place that exhibited any signs of a rendezvous.

This fact confirmed the suspicions of the law-

—10

abiding portion of the community, that there existed in their midst and neighboring settlements on Ute creek an organized band of "road agents," who started out only on favorable opportunities for carrying on their nefarious purposes.

It was believed by many that persons residing in Elizabethtown kept watch, advised their partners in this crime at Ute creek at what time a large shipment of gold would probably be made, and the number of passengers, with their names, the coach would carry.

Wal. absented himself from the camp a day or two at a time, and it began to be murmured that he could tell, if he would, a great deal concerning these systematic robberies. It was even hinted that he not only directly aided and abetted the attacks on the coach, but took an active part himself.

He was very reticent on the subject, and it was a fact commented upon by nearly every one in camp, that after an absence of two or three days he would invariably turn up the very morning after a robbery with a load of wood for sale, and as demurely ride through town on his little wagon as if such a thing as an attack on the coach the day before had never taken place.

Of course no positive proof of his complicity

could be obtained, yet it was generally believed that he belonged to the gang.

The man who kept the principal saloon was well known throughout the Territory, not only on account of his size and weight but also in consequence of his insatiable thirst for "bug-juice" and his dexterous manipulation of the cards; and he was withal a law-abiding citizen. He would tolerate nothing that was not strictly "regular" in the eye of the law. He wouldn't steal a horse, or carry off a red-hot stove, but woe to the unfortunate and confiding individual who sat down to his game with the expectation of leaving with a cent in his clothes.

His thorough knowledge of monte, faro, poker, and other "genteel" games, made him as much a terror behind the green-covered table as a pack of highway robbers. While he would not hesitate to fleece some unsuspecting victim in a "gentlemanly" game, he had no sympathy with any lawbreaker or "road agent" who would halt a man for his money without the farcical proceeding of having a little bout of cards to win it honorably.

One afternoon while the robberies of the mail coach were at their height, three or four broken-down gamblers sauntered into his saloon and commenced to discuss the last depredation, and the *modus operandi* of the efficient "agents."

Prominent among the group was Wal.; each had his theory to advance, and each expressed it freely.   .

The barkeeper said: "Don't yer understand," — a favorite expression when excited —"don't yer understand, the —— rascals don't live a great ways from this camp, and I would n't wonder if a few of them — don't yer understand — are right in sight of this shebang now, don't yer understand. I hain't got no sympathy for any such work — don't yer understand — and would help hang every mother's son of 'em, don't yer understand!"

Old Sam Bartlett expressed it as "his opinion that Reub. Jones, of Ute creek, knowed all about it, and was at the head of the gang."

Wal. put in his oar occasionally, but from his remarks it was apparent that his sympathy was rather in favor of that style of robbing than "stealing it through a —— old faro-box."

Words waxed high, and it was evident there "was going to be a difficult," as Kit Carson used to say.

The proprietor saw that trouble would ensue if the conversation was not dropped; so, desirous of putting an end to it, he turned to Wal. and said: "Wal., we've had enough of this—so come on and have a drink and go home."

Wal. accepted the invitation, and with a closing remark that "he considered the robbers were a —— sight better than some of the genteel thieves who lived right in camp," he walked up to the bar, while the owner from behind said, "Wal., what will you have?"

"I'll take whisky in mine," answered Wal.

Glass and bottle were set out, and while the proprietor was mixing a toddy beneath the bar for himself, Wal. seized the bottle, poured his glass full to the brim, then deliberately emptied it on the counter with the remark, "If you don't like that, why, then take your change anyway you want it," at the same instant putting his hand on his hip as if in the act of drawing his pistol.

As quick as thought, the proprietor, knowing the desperate character of the man he had to deal with, seized a pistol from behind the bar, leveled it, fired, and Wal. fell dead; then, immediately stepping from where he was to the front, pistol in hand, he emptied the remaining chambers of his revolver into the prostrate body.

He gave himself up at once; an examination was shortly held before the alcalde, where all the facts were elicited, and the verdict of the jury was, "Justifiable homicide."

Thus ended the career of Wal. Henderson, whose bones are reposing on the little hill above the now abandoned camp, where a score or more of others lie who went the same way.

PAWNEE ROCK has probably been the scene of a hundred fights, and a volume could be written in relation to it. Kit Carson, one night some years ago, when camped half-way up the rugged sides of "Old Baldy" in the Raton Range, told in his peculiarly expressive way, among other border reminiscences, the following little story, the incidents of which occurred long years ago.

The night was cold, although midsummer, and we were huddled around a little fire of pine-knots, more than eight thousand feet above the level of the sea, close to the snow limit. We had left Maxwell's early in the morning to trace a quartz lead that cropped out near the mouth of the copper mine worked by him, and night overtook us many miles from the ranch; so we concluded to remain on the mountain until daylight. We had no blankets, and of course had to sit up through the long hours; and as it was terribly cold, we made a fire, filled our pipes, and spun yarns to keep awake. Our lunch that we had brought was all eaten about noon,—so we were supperless as well; but a swift cold mountain stream ran close to our little camp, and we took a swallow of that occasionally, which served the place of a meal.

Kit (the General, as every one called him) was in a good humor for talking, and we naturally took advantage of this to draw him out,—for usually he was the most reticent of men in relation to his own exploits. The night was pretty dark, there was no moon, and our fire of dry knots blazed up beautifully every time the two Indians, whom we had appointed to this special duty, threw a fresh armful on. The flames cast their weird and fanciful shadows on the side of the mountain, and contrasted curiously with the inky blackness all around below us, while far above could be seen the dim outline of "Old Baldy's" scarred and weather-beaten crest—crag piled upon crag, until they seemed to touch the starlit sky.

For an hour or two the conversation was confined to the probabilities of gold being found in paying quantities in the mountains and gulches of the range; and when the interest on that subject flagged, Maxwell having made a casual remark in relation to some peak near by, just discernible in the darkness, and connecting the locality with some trouble he had had ten or a dozen years before with the Indians, his reminiscences opened Kit Carson's mouth, and he said he remembered one of the "worst difficults" a man ever got into; so he made a fresh corn-shuck cigarette and told us the following about Pawnee Rock, which he said had been written up years ago, and that he had a paper containing it (which he afterward gave me), and which, with what Kit related orally that night, is here presented:

"It was old Jim Gibson — poor fellow, he went under in a fight with the Utes over twenty years ago, and his bones are bleaching somewhere in the dark cañons of the range, or on the slopes of the Spanish Peaks. He used to tell of a scrimmage he and another fellow had on the Arkansas with the Kiowas, in 1836.

"Jim and his partner, Bill something-or-other, — I disremember his name now, — had been trapping up in the Powder river country during the winter, with unusual good luck. The beaver was mighty thick in the whole Yellowstone region in them days, and Jim and Bill got an early start on their journey for the

River* that spring. You see they expected to
sell their truck in Weston, Mo., which was the
principal trading-point on the River then.
They walked the whole distance — over fifteen
hundred miles — driving three good mules before
them, on which their plunder was packed, and
they got along well enough until they struck the
Arkansas river at Pawnee Rock. Here they met
a war party of about sixty Kiowas, who treed
them on the Rock. Jim and Bill were noto-
riously brave, and both dead shots.

"Before they reached the Rock, to which they
were driven, they killed ten of the Kiowas, and
had not received a scratch. They had plenty of
powder and a pouchful of bullets each. They
also had a couple of jack-rabbits for food in case
of a siege, and the perpendicular walls of the
Rock made them a natural fortification — an almost impregnable one.

"They succeeded in securely picketing their
animals on the west side of the Rock, where they
could protect them by their unerring rifles——
but the story of the fight must be told in Jim's
own way; he was a pretty well educated fellow,
and had been to college, I believe, in his younger
days,— lost the gal he was going to marry, or had

---

*In the old days, among the plainsmen and mountaineers, whenever
"the River" was alluded to it was understood to mean the Missouri

some bad luck or other, and took to the prairies when he was about twenty. I will try to tell it as near as he did as possible:

"After the durned red cusses had treed us, they picked up their dead and packed them to their camp at the mouth of the creek a little piece off. In a few moments back they all came, mounted, with all their fixings and war-paint on. Then they commenced to circle around us, coming closer, Indian fashion, every time, till they got within easy rifle range, when they slung themselves on the fore sides of their ponies, and in that position opened on us. Their arrows fell like a hail-storm around us for a few minutes, but as good luck would have it, none of them struck. I was afraid that first of all, they would attempt to kill our mules; but I suppose they thought they had the dead wood on us, and the mules would come mighty handy for their own use after our scalps were dangling at their belts. But we were taking in all the chances. Bill kept his eyes skinned, and whenever he saw a stray leg or head he drew a bead on it, and *thug!* over tumbled its owner every time, with a yell of rage.

- "Whenever they attempted to carry off their dead, that was the moment we took the advantage, and we poured it into them as soon as they rallied for that purpose, with telling effect. We wasted no shots; we had now only about forty bullets between us, and the miserable cusses seemed thick as ever.

"The sun was nearly down by this time, and at dark they did not seem anxious to renew the fight that night, but I could see their mounted patrols at a respectable distance on every side, watching to prevent our escape. I took advantage of the darkness to go down and get a few buffalo-chips to cook our supper, for we were mighty hungry, and to change the animals to where they could get a little more grass,—though for that matter it was nearly up to a man's head all over the bottom.

"I got back to our camp on top without any trouble, when we made a little fire and cooked a rabbit. We had to go without water, and so did the animals; though we did not mind the want of it so much ourselves, we pitied the mules, which had had none since we broke camp in the morning. It was of no use to worry about it, though; the nearest water was in the spring at the Indian camp, and it would be certain death to attempt to get there.

"I was afraid the red devils would fire the prairie in the morning and endeavor to smoke

or burn us out.   The grass was just in a condition
to make a lively blaze, and we might escape the
flames,—and we might not.

"We watched with eager eyes for the first
gray streaks of dawn that would usher in another
day—perhaps the last for us.

"The next morning's sun had scarcely peeped
above the horizon, when, with an infernal yell,
the Indians broke for the Rock, and we knew
some new project had entered their heads.

"The wind was springing up pretty fresh, and
nature seemed to conspire with the red devils if
they really meant to burn us out,—and I had no
doubt now from their movements that that was
what they intended.   The darned cusses kept at
such a respectful distance from our rifles that it
chafed us to know that we could not stop the infernal throats of some of them with our bullets;
but we had to choke our rage and watch events
closely.

"I took occasion during the lull in hostilities
to crawl down to where the mules were and shift
them to the east side of the Rock, where the wall
was the highest, so that the flames and smoke
might possibly pass by them without so much
danger as on the exposed other side.

"I succeeded in doing this, and also in tearing

away the grass for several yards around the animals, and was just starting back when Bill called
out, ' —— 'em, they 've fired the prairie! '

"I reached the top of the Rock in a moment,
and took in at a glance what was coming. The
spectacle for a short interval was indescribably
grand. The sun was shining with all the powers
of its rays on the huge clouds of smoke as they
rolled down from the north, tinting them with a
glorious crimson. I had barely time to get under
shelter of a projecting point of the Rock when the
wind and smoke swept down to the ground, and
instantly we were enveloped in the darkness of
midnight. We could not discern a single object,
neither Indians, horses, the prairie, nor sun — and
what a terrible wind! I have never experienced
its equal in violence since. We stood breathless,
and clinging to the projection of our little mass
of rock did not realize that the fire was so near
until we were struck in the face by the burning
buffalo-chips that were carried toward us with
the rapidity of the wind. I was really scared; it
seemed as if we must suffocate. But we were
saved miraculously. The sheet of flame passed
us twenty yards away, as the wind fortunately
shifted the moment the fire reached the Rock.
Yet the darkness was so perfect we did not see the

flame; we only knew that we were safe, as the
clear sky greeted us behind the dense cloud of
smoke.

"Two of the Indians and their horses were
caught in their own trap, and perished miserably.
They had attempted to reach the east side of the
Rock where the mules were, either to cut them
loose or crawl up on us while bewildered in the
smoke, if we escaped death. But they had proceeded only a few rods on their little expedition
when the terrible darkness of the smoke-cloud
overtook them.

"All the game on the prairie which the fire
swept over was killed too. Only a few buffaloes
were visible in that region before the fire, but
even they were killed. The path of this horrible
passage of flames, as we learned afterward, was
marked all along with the crisped and blackened
carcasses of wolves, coyotes, turkeys, grouse, and
every variety of small birds. Indeed, it seemed
as if no living thing it met had escaped its fury.

"The fire assumed such gigantic proportions
and moved with such rapidity before the terrible
wind, that even the Arkansas river did not check
its path for a moment, and we watched it carried
across as readily as if the river had not been in
the way. This fearful prairie-fire traveled at the

rate of eight miles in fifteen minutes, and was probably the most violent in its features that ever visited that country. It was the most sublime picture I ever looked upon, and for a moment it made us forget our perilous position.

"My first thought, after the danger had passed, was of the poor mules. I crawled down to where they were, and found them badly singed but not seriously hurt. I thought, 'So far so good;' our mules and traps were all right, so we took courage and began to think we should get out of the nasty scrape in some way or other.

"In the meantime the Indians, with the exception of four or five left to guard the Rock so we could not escape, had gone back to their camp on the creek, and were evidently concocting some new scheme to capture or kill us.

"We waited patiently two or three hours for the development of events, snatching a little sleep by turns, until the sun was about four hours high, when the Indians commenced their infernal howling again, and we knew they had hit upon something; so we were on the alert in a moment to discover it, and eucher them if possible.

"The devils this time had tied all their horses together, covered them with branches of trees that they had cut on the creek, packed all the lodge-skins on these, and then, driving the living breast-works before them toward us, themselves followed close behind on foot. They kept moving slowly but surely in the direction of the Rock, and matters began to look serious for us once more.

"'Bill put his hand in mine now, and said, 'Jim, now by —— we got to fight; we hain't done nothin' yit; this means business.'

"I said, 'You're right, Bill, old fellow; but they can't get us alive. Our plan is to kill their ponies and make the cusses halt.'

"As I spoke, Bill—who was one of the best shots on the Plains—kind o' threw his eye care-lessly along the bar'l of his rifle, and one of the ponies tumbled over on the blackened sod. One of the Indians ran out to cut him loose, as I expected, and I took him clean off his feet without a groan. Quicker than it takes me to tell it, we had stretched out twelve of them on the prairie, and we made it so hot for them that they got out of range, and were apparently holding a council of war.

"We kept watching the devils' movements, for we knew they would soon be up to some confounded trick. The others did not make their appearance immediately from behind their living breastworks, so we fired two shots apiece into the

—11

horses, killing three of them and throwing the whole outfit into confusion.

"We soon stopped their little plan, and they had now only. the dead bodies of the ponies we had killed, to protect them, for the others had broken loose and stampeded off to camp. It was getting pretty hot for Mr. Indian now, who was on foot and in easy range of our rifles. We cleaned out one or two more while they were gradually pulling themselves out of range, when of course we had to stop firing. The Indians started off to their camp again, and during the lull in hostilities we took an account of stock. We found we had used up all our ammunition except three or four loads, and despair seemed to hover over us once more.

"In a few moments we were surprised to see one of the warriors come out alone from camp, and tearing off a piece of his white blanket, he boldly walked toward the Rock. Coming up within hearing, he asked if we would have a talk with him. We told him yes, but did not look for any good results from it. We could not expect anything less than torture if we allowed ourselves to be taken alive, so we determined not to be caught in any trap. We knew we had done them too much damage to expect any mercy, so we prepared to die in the fight, if we must die.

"We beckoned the young buck nearer and listened to what he had to say. He said they were part of White Buffalo's band of Kiowas; that the war chief who was here with them was O-ton-son-e-var ('a herd of buffaloes'), and that he wanted us to come to the camp; that we were 'heap brave'; we should be kindly treated, and that the tribe would adopt us. They were on their way to the Sioux country north of the Platte; that they were going there to steal horses from the Sioux. They expected a fight, and wanted us to help them.

O-TON-SON-E-VAR.

"Bill and myself knew the darned Indians too well to swallow their chaff, so we told them that we could not think of accepting their terms; that we were on our way to the Missouri, and meant to get there or die in the attempt; that we did not fear them,—the white man's God would take care of us; and that if that was all they had to talk about, he could go back and tell his party they could begin the fight again as soon as they pleased.

"He started back, and before he had reached the creek they came out and met him, had a confab, and then began the attack on us at once. We made each of our four loads tell, and then stood at bay, almost helpless and defenseless: we were at the mercy of the savages, and they understood our situation as quickly as ourselves.

"We were now thrown upon our last resource — the boy's-play of throwing stones. As long as we could find detached pieces of rock they did not dare to make an assault, and while we were still wondering what next, the white flag appeared again and demanded another talk. We knew that now we had to come to terms, and make up our minds to accept anything that savored of reason and our lives, trusting to the future to escape if they kept us as prisoners.

"'The Kiowas are not prisoners, and they know brave men,' said the Indian; 'we will not kill you, though the prairie-grass is red with the blood of our warriors that have died by your hands.

We will give you a chance for your lives, and let
you prove that the Great Spirit of the white man
is powerful, and can save you.   Behold,' said the
Indian, pointing with an arrow to a solitary cot-
tonwood on the banks of the Arkansas, a mile or
more away, 'you must go there, and one of you
shall run the knife-gauntlet from that tree two
hundred steps of the chief out toward the prairie.
If the one who runs escapes, both are free, for the
Great Spirit has willed it.   O-ton-son-e-var has
said it, and the words of the Kiowa are true.'

" ' When must the trial take place ? ' said I.

" ' When the sun begins to shine upon the western edge of the Rock,' replied the Indian.

" 'Say to your chief we accept the challenge
and will be ready,' said Bill, motioning the young
warrior away. 'I am sure I can win,' said he,
' and can save both our lives. O-ton-son-e-var
will keep his word—I know him.'   .

" ' Bill,' said I, ' I shall run that race, not you ; '
and taking him by the hand I told him that if he
saw I was going to fail, to watch his chance, and
in the excitement of the moment mount one of
their horses and fly toward Bent's Fort; he could
escape—he was young; it made no difference
with me—my life was not worth much, but he
had all before him.   .

" 'No,' replied Bill, 'my heart is set on this; I traveled the same race once before when the Apaches got me, and their knives never struck me once. I ask this favor as my life, for I have a presentiment that it is only I can win. I know how to get every advantage of them. So say no more.'

"The sun had scarcely gilded that portion of the dark line of the Rock that juts out boldly toward the western horizon, before all the warriors, with O-ton-son-e-var at their head, marched silently toward.the tree and beckoned us to come.

PACER'S SON—CHIEF OF ALL
THE APACHES.

"Quickly we were on the prairie beside them, when they opened a space, and we walked in their center without exchanging a word. There were only thirty left of that band of sixty proud warriors who had commenced the attack on us the day before, and I could see by the scowls with which they regarded us,. and by the convulsive clutching at their knives by the younger ones, that it was only the presence and power of O-ton-son-e-var which prevented them from taking summary vengeance upon us.

"As soon as we reached the tree, O-ton-son-e-var paced the two hundred steps, and arranged his warriors on either side, who in a moment stripped themselves to the waist, and each seizing his long scalping-knife, and bracing himself, held it high over his head, so as to strike a blow that would carry it to the hilt at once.

"The question of who should be their victim was settled immediately, for as I stepped forward to face that narrow passage of probable death, the chief signaled me back with an impulsive gesture not to be misunderstood, and pointing to Bill, told him to prepare himself for the bloody trial.

"I attempted to protest, and was urging my most earnest words, when O-ton-son-e-var said he had decided, and 'the young man must run,' adding that 'even a drop of blood from any one of the knives meant death to both.'

"Each savage stood firm, with his glittering blade reflecting the rays of the evening sun, and on each hard cold face a determination to have the heart's blood of their victim.

"The case seemed almost hopeless — it was truly a race for life; and as Bill prepared himself I wished ourselves back on the Rock, with only as many good bullets as the number of red devils who stood before us, the very impersonation of all the hatred of the detestable red man.

"How well I remember the coolness and confidence of Bill! He could not have been more calm if he had been stripping for a foot-race for fun. He had perfect faith in the result, and when O-ton-son-e-var motioned to commence the fearful trial, Bill spoke to me, but I could not answer — my grief was too great.

"He stripped to his drawers, and standing there awaiting the signal, naked from the belt up, he was the picture of the noblest manhood I ever saw. He tightened his belt, and stood for a few seconds looking, with compressed lips, down the double row of savages, as they stood, face to face, gloating on their victim. It seemed like an age to me, and when the signal came I was forced by an irresistible power to look upon the scene.

"At the instant Bill darted like a flash of lightning from the foot of the tree; on rushed the devils with their gleaming blades, yelling, and crowding one another, and cutting at poor Bill with all the rage of their revengeful nature.

But he evaded all their horrible efforts — now
tossing a savage here and another there, now almost creeping like a snake at their feet, then like
a wildcat he would jump through the line, dash-
ing the knives out of their hands, till at last,
with a single spring, he passed almost twenty feet
beyond the mark where the chief stood.

"We were saved, and when the disappointed
savages were crowding around him I rushed in
and threw myself in his arms. The chief motioned the impatient warriors away, and with
sullen footsteps followed them.

"In a few moments we slowly retraced our way
to the Rock, where, taking our mules, we pushed
on in the direction of the Missouri. We camped
on the bank of the Arkansas that night, only a
few miles from the terrible Rock; and while we
were resting around our little fire of buffalo-
chips, and our animals were quietly nibbling the
dried grass at our feet, we could still hear the
Kiowas chanting the death-song as they buried
their lost warriors under the blackened sod of the
prairie."

SHERIDAN'S ROOST.

GENERAL P. H. SHERIDAN.

LESS than a third of a century ago the western half of southern Kansas and the whole region beyond, including the historical Washita, where General Custer defeated the famous chief of the Cheyennes, Black Kettle, was the habitat of our noblest indigenous bird, the wild turkey. The dense woods bordering all the streams were full of them, for the wild turkey makes his haunts in the timber.

Having visited that once favorite winter rendezvous of the Cheyennes and Kiowas during the early spring, and stood again on the ground where

Sheridan and Custer in their celebrated campaign of 1868–9 so effectually subdued the Indians that the Western frontier has ever since been exempt from their bloody raids, the recollection of many exciting wild-turkey hunts by the two incomparable soldiers came vividly to my mind. I remember distinctly, as if it were but a week since, how during that winter campaign of nearly thirty years ago the troops sent into the field against the allied hostile tribes subsisted for days on wild turkey — luckily for them, too, as they were almost without a ration, and would have suffered in a greater degree than they did but for the presence of great flocks of the delicious birds.

In addition to the stern necessity of securing them, shooting them under the brilliant mid-continent full moon that nowhere else shines more intensely, afforded an immense amount of sport to both officers and enlisted men, divesting their weary march through that then desolate region of its terrible monotony. General Sheridan was a crack shot, recognized as an expert in pheasant-hunting when a young lieutenant in the wilds of Oregon, long before the Civil War, and where large game roamed in immense numbers through the vast forests. Then the height of the embryo

great General's ambition was that he might at-
tain the rank of Major before he died!

There is a large body of timber on the North
Fork of the Canadian river in the Indian Territory, about sixty miles directly south of the
Kansas line, known as "Sheridan's Roost"—so
marked on the maps. It was there that General
Sheridan with Custer bagged an almost incredible
number of wild turkeys while camping on the
now historic spot.

It was on the afternoon of one of the last days
in the month of December, 1868, when the tired
command found itself encamped very near an immense turkey roost. Both Sheridan and Custer,
as soon as they had dismounted from their horses,
made the fortuitous discovery and grasped the
important situation: an abundance of food for
the half-starved troopers and a relief to the ennui
and tiresome routine of the monotonous march
through the seemingly interminable sand-dunes
so frequent in that region.

In order that the necessities of the command
and the anticipated sport might not be thwarted
by a general firing of the rank and file under the
excitement natural to the average soldier, Sheridan immediately issued an order that no one —
officer, enlisted man, or civilian — should leave

camp without his permission. He was well aware
of the fact that if any prowling around was allowed, the now absent birds would not return to
their accustomed resting-place when night came
on.

The whole command was restless, anxious and
impatient for hours, waiting for the seemingly
tardy sun to set. At last, after two hours of sus-
pense, the fading rays began to gild the summits
of the low range of hills west of the camp. Then,
just as the twilight curve reached the horizon, the
General, with Custer and several other officers
whom he had chosen as companions, left their
camp-fire of blazing logs and sauntered slowly
into the thick woods where it had been discovered
early in the afternoon that the coveted birds were
in the habit of congregating to roost.

Arriving at the very center of the vast sleeping-
place, at the suggestion of General Custer each
gentleman took a position on the ground, separated from each other some distance, to watch
from their individual vantage-point until the
moment should come for the birds to seek their
accustomed resting-place.

They did not have to wait long. Before it had
grown fairly dark, two or three flocks containing
at least two hundred of the bronzed beauties came

walking stealthily down the sheltered ravines leading out into the broad bottom where the great trees stood in aggregated clumps, under whose shadows General Sheridan had first observed the unmistakable signs of a vast roost. At the head of each flock, as it unsuspiciously advanced, strutted a magnificent male bird in all the arrogance of his leadership, and on whose bronzed plumage the soft full moon which had just risen, glinted like a calcium light as its golden rays sifted through the interstices of the bare limbs of the winter-garbed forest.

When the leader had arrived at the spot where his charge had been accustomed to roost, he suddenly halted, glanced all around him for a few seconds, then seemingly satisfied that everything was right, he gave the signal—a sharp, quick, shrill whistle. At that instant every bird with one accord and a tremendous fluttering of wings, raised itself and alighted in the loftiest branches of the tallest trees.

In a few moments more, many more flocks arrived and went through exactly the same evolutions as the first two, when, having settled themselves for an undisturbed slumber, General Sheridan gave the word for the slaughter to begin. Each officer then began to shoot on his own account, and the turkeys fell like the leaves in October. The stupid birds not killed at the first fusillade did not seem to have sense enough to get out of harm's way: they flew from tree to tree at every shot, persistently remaining in the immediate vicinity of their roost with all the characteristic idiocy of a sage-hen, which, according to my observation, has less sense than any other bird that flies.

It was soon time that all honest men whether "in camp or court" were in bed, but the two famous generals and their companions, so exciting was the rare sport, did not leave until the moon was far down the western horizon.

They then returned to the friendly fires near their tents and counted the number of birds which had fallen under the accurate aim of those engaged. It was discovered they had bagged nearly a hundred of the magnificent bronzed creatures, of which Sheridan had killed the lion's share.

From that midnight incident in the beginning of that eventful winter on the Great Plains, "Sheridan's Roost" received its name; the spot became classic, and will go down to the generations yet unborn with its suggestive title.

Although the majority of the birds stuck to the vicinity of their roost, yet continually slaughtered by the unerring rifles of the officers, appearing to be too senseless to avert their doom by flying off, some, however, did go recklessly into the very camp of the troopers. The picket-line had long since been stretched, and preparations for the men's evening meal, scanty as it was to be, were fairly under way. But the cooks, expecting that some of the birds would, frightened as they evidently were by the deadly shots of the officers, fly into camp in their bewilderment, were a little slow and perfunctory, anticipating that the bill of fare, that night at least, would vary materially from the customary horse-meat and hard-tack.

Sure enough, several large flocks "rounded up" in full view of the command just as the firing commenced. It was a curious as well as a remarkable scene to watch the evident surprise and discomfiture of the birds to discover the whole ground usurped by the soldiers; they were bewildered beyond the power of description. They stood still for a few moments seemingly paralyzed, but as other flocks began to enter the camp, all in the quickest imaginable time flew into the tallest trees. At this juncture every soldier was seized with a desire to shoot, and a fusillade began right there, resulting in tumbling off the

huge limbs fifty or more of the crazed birds. Of
course, the remainder were driven away from
their roost, until the very air was black with the
alarmed and bewildered turkeys.

As the dark night came on, not knowing where
to go, and failing to seek another quiet roosting-
place, back they all came, but in increased numbers, evidently determined to roost there or
nowhere. The air was filled and the ground covered with wild turkeys. They were dazed at the
turn affairs had taken, and great flocks ran, bewildered, right among the soldiers and wagons of
the supply train. Then was a scene enacted such
as perhaps was never before witnessed, nor has
it since, in all probability. All the dogs in the
command—and there was every breed and every
size in the camp, for the average American soldier
loves a dog and keeps as many as he can—joined
in the pandemonium that ensued in the chase
after the frightened birds, accompanied by a
fusillade which in point of rapidity and volume
of noise would have done credit to a corps in a
general engagement.

Some casualties occurred, of course, but no lives
were lost save that of a horse, under the following circumstances: One of the troopers of the
Nineteenth Kansas Cavalry, who was in the act

—12

of leading his animal to the picket-line at the
height of the chase, was somewhat astonished to
find that his faithful beast failed to respond to
the tugging at his halter-strap as he endeavored
to bring him to the stretched rope, and looking
around to discover the cause, the excited trooper
saw the unfortunate animal on the ground, dead,
having been instantly killed by an erratic ball!

There was great feasting in the command that
night. Never did turkey taste so delicious as did
the magnificent birds served in every conceivable
style at that late meal in camp on the classic
Washita, to the half-famished soldiers of the
famous Seventh Cavalry and the gallant boys of
the Kansas regiment.

THE PASSING OF THE BUFFALO.

T O the old trapper and
hunter of the palmy
days of '68 and '70,
I dedicate this chap-
ter. That time is
now faded into the
past, and so far faded,
indeed, that the pres-
ent generation knows
not its sympathy nor
its sentiment.

The buffalo—as
my thoughts turn to
the past, the memory
of their "age" (if I
may so call it) crowds
upon me. I remember when the eye could not
measure their numbers. I saw a herd delay a
railroad train from 9 o'clock in the morning until
5 o'clock in the afternoon. Countless millions,
divided by its leaders and captains like an immense army! How many millions there were,

179

none could guess. On each side of us, and as far as we could see — our vision was limited only by the extended horizon of the flat prairie — the whole vast area was black with the surging mass of affrighted animals, as they rushed onward to the south in a mad stampede.

At another time Gens. Sheridan, Custer, Sully, and myself rode through another and larger one, for three consecutive days. This was in the fall of 1868. It seems almost impossible to those who have seen them, as numerous apparently as the sands of the seashore, feeding on the illimitable natural pasturage of the Great Plains, that the buffalo should have become practically extinct. When I look back only twenty-five years and recall the fact that they swarmed in countless numbers even then as far east as Fort Harker, only 200 miles west from the Missouri river, I ask myself, "Have they all disappeared?" And yet, such is the fact. Two causes can be assigned for this great hecatomb: First, the demand for their hides, which brought about a great invasion of hunters into this region; and second, the crowds of thoughtless tourists who crossed the continent for the mere novelty and pleasure of the trip. This latter class heartlessly killed for the excitement of the new experience as they rode along in

the cars at a low rate of speed, often never touching a particle of the flesh of their victims, or
possessing themselves of a single robe.

The former, numbering hundreds of old frontiersmen, all expert shots, with thousands of
novices, the pioneer settlers on the public do-
main, day after day for years made it a lucrative
business to kill for the robes alone, a market
for which had suddenly sprung up all over the
country.

The beginning of the end was marked by the
completion of the Kansas Pacific across the Plains
to the foot-hills of the Rockies in 1868, this being
the western limit of the buffalo range.

In 1872 a writer in "The Buffalo Land" said:

"Probably the most cruel of all bison-shooting
pastime is that of firing from the cars. During
certain periods in the spring and fall, when the
large herds are crossing the Kansas Pacific Railroad, the trains run for a hundred miles or more
among countless thousands of the shaggy mon-
archs of the Plains. The bison has a strange and
entirely unaccountable instinct or habit which
leads it to attempt crossing in front of any moving object near it. It frequently happened, in the
time of the old stages, that the driver had to rein
up his horses until the herd which he had started

had crossed the road ahead of him. To accomplish this feat, if the object of their fright was moving rapidly, the animals would often run for miles.

"When the iron horse comes rushing into their solitudes, and snorting out his fierce alarms, the herds, though perhaps half a mile from his path, will lift their heads and gaze intently for a few minutes toward the object thus approaching them with a roar which causes the earth to tremble, and enveloped in a white cloud that streams further and higher than the dust of the old stage-coach ever did; and then, having determined its course, instead of fleeing back to the distant valleys, away they go, charging over the ridge across which the iron rails lie, apparently determined to cross in front of the locomotive at all hazards. The rate per mile of the passenger trains is slow upon the Plains, and hence it often happens that the cars and buffaloes will be side by side for a mile or two, the brutes abandoning the effort to cross only when their foe has emerged entirely ahead. During these races the car windows are opened, and numerous breech-loaders fling hundreds of bullets among the densely crowded and fast-flying masses. Many of the poor animals fall, and more go off to die in the ravines. The train speeds on, and the act is repeated every few miles until Buffalo Land is passed."

Almost with prophetic eye he continued:

"Let this slaughter continue for ten years, and the bison of the American continent will become extinct. The number of valuable robes and pounds of meat which would thus be lost to us and posterity, will run too far into the millions to be easily calculated. All over the Plains, lying in disgusting masses of putrefaction along valley and hill, are strewn immense carcasses of wantonly slain buffalo. They line the Kansas Pacific road for two hundred miles."

A great herd of buffaloes on the Plains in the early days, when one could approach near enough without disturbing it to quietly watch its organization, and the apparent discipline which its leaders seemed to exact, was a very curious sight. Among the striking features of the spectacle was the apparently uniform manner in which the immense mass of shaggy animals moved; there was constancy of action indicating a degree of intelligence to be found only in the most intelligent of the brute creation. Frequently the larger herd was broken up into many smaller ones, that traveled relatively close together, each

led by an independent master. Perhaps only a
few rods marked the dividing-line between them,
but it was always unmistakably plain, and each
moved synchronously in the direction in which
all were going.

The leadership of the herd was attained only by
hard struggles for the place; once reached, however, the victor was immediately recognized, and
kept his authority until some new aspirant over-
came him, or he became superannuated and was
driven out of the herd to meet his inevitable fate,
a prey to those ghouls of the desert, the gray
wolves.

In the event of a stampede, every animal of the
separate yet consolidated herds rushed off together,
as if all had gone mad at once; for the buffalo,
like the Texas steer, mule, or domestic horse, stampedes on the slightest provocation — frequently
without any assignable cause. Sometimes the simplest affair will start the whole herd: a prairie-
dog barking at the entrance of his burrow, a
shadow of one of themselves or that of a passing
cloud, is sufficient to make them run for miles as
if a real and dangerous enemy were at their heels.

Stampedes were a great source of profit to the
Indians of the Plains. The Comanches were particularly expert and daring in this kind of rob-

bery.   They even trained their horses to run from
one point to another, in expectation of the coming
of the wagon trains on the trail.   When a camp
was made that was nearly in range, they turned
their trained animals loose, which at once flew
across the prairie, passing through the herd and
penetrating the very corrals of their victims.   All
of the picketed horses and mules would endeavor
to follow these decoys, and were invariably led
right into the haunts of the Indians, who easily
secured them.   Young horses and mules were
easily frightened; and in the confusion which
generally ensued, great injury was frequently
done to the runaways themselves.

At times when the herd was very large, the
horses scattered over the prairie and were irrevocably lost; and such as did not become wild fell
a prey to the wolves.   That fate was very frequently the lot of stampeded horses bred in the
States, they not having been trained by a prairie
life to care for themselves.   Instead of stopping
and bravely fighting off the bloodthirsty beasts,
they would run.   Then the whole pack were sure
to leave the bolder animals and make for the runaways, which they seldom failed to overtake and
dispatch.

Like an army, a herd of buffaloes put out ve-

dettes to give the alarm in case anything beyond
the ordinary occurred. These sentinels were always to be seen in groups of four, five, or even
six, at some distance from the main body. When
they saw something approaching that the herd
should beware of or get away from, they started
on the run directly for the center of the great
mass of their peacefully grazing congeners. Meanwhile, the young bulls were on duty as sentinels on
the edge of the main herd, watching the vedettes;
the moment the latter made for the center, the
former raised their heads, and in the peculiar
manner of their species gazed all around and
sniffed the air as if they could smell both the
danger and its direction. Should there be something which their instinct told them to guard
against, the leader took his position in front, the
cows and calves crowded in the center, while the
rest of the males gathered on the flanks and in
the rear, indicating a gallantry that might be
imitated at times by the *genus homo*.

Generally, buffalo went to their drinking-place
but once a day, and that late in the afternoon.
Then they ambled along, following each other in
single file, which accounts for the many trails on
the Plains, always ending at some stream or lake.
They frequently traveled twenty or thirty miles

for water; so the trails leading to it were often worn to the depth of a foot or more.

That curious depression so frequently seen on the Great Plains, called a "buffalo wallow," is caused in this wise: The huge animals paw and lick the salty, alkaline earth, and when once the sod is broken the loose soil drifts away under the constant action of the wind. Then, year after year, through more pawing, licking, rolling and wallowing by the animals, the wind wafts more of the soil away, and soon there is a considerable hole in the prairie.

Many an old trapper and hunter's life has been saved by following a buffalo trail when he was suffering from thirst. The buffalo wallows usually retain a great quantity of water, and they have often saved the lives of whole companies of cavalry, both men and horses.

There was, however, a stranger and more wonderful spectacle to be seen every recurring spring during the reign of ·the buffalo, soon after the grass had started. There were circles trodden bare on the Plains, thousands — yes, millions — of them, which the early travelers, who did not divine their cause, called "fairy rings." From the first of April until the middle of May was the wet season; you could depend upon its recurrence almost as certainly as on the sun and moon rising at the proper time. This was also the calving period of the buffalo, as they, unlike our domestic animals, only rutted during a single month; consequently the cows all calved during a certain time; this was the wet month, and as there were a great many gray wolves that roamed singly or in immense packs over the whole prairie region, the bulls, in their regular beats, kept guard over the cows while in the act of parturition, and drove the wolves away, walking in a ring around the females at a short distance, and thus forming the curious circles.

In every herd at each recurring season there were always ambitious young bulls that came to their majority, so to speak, and these were ever ready to test their claims for the leadership; so that it may be safely stated that a month rarely passed without a bloody battle between them for the supremacy—though, strangely enough, the struggle seldom resulted in the death of either combatant.

Perhaps there is no animal in which maternal love is more strongly developed than in the buffalo cow; she is as dangerous with a calf by her side as a she-grizzly with cubs.

The buffalo bull that has outlived his usefulness

is one of the most pitiable objects in the whole
range of natural history. Old age has probably
been decided in the economy of buffalo life as the
unpardonable sin. Abandoned to his fate, he may
be discovered in his dreary isolation, near some
stream or lake, where it does not tax him too se-
verely to find good grass; for he is now feeble,
and exertion an impossibility. In this new stage
of his existence he seems to have completely lost
his courage. Frightened at his own shadow, or
the rustling of a leaf, he is the very incarnation
of nervousness and suspicion. Gregarious in his
habits from birth, solitude, foreign to his whole
nature, has changed him into a new creature;
and his inherent terror of the most trivial things
is intensified to such a degree that if a man were
compelled to undergo such constant alarm, it
would probably drive him insane in less than a
week. Nobody ever saw one of these miserable
and forlorn creatures dying a natural death, or
even heard of such an occurrence. The cowardly
coyote and the gray wolf had already marked
him for their own; and they rarely missed their
calculations.

Rising suddenly to the top of a divide with a
party of friends in 1866, we saw standing below
us in the valley an old buffalo bull, the very pic-

ture of despair. Surrounding him were seven gray wolves in the act of challenging him to mortal combat. The poor beast, undoubtedly realizing the hopelessness of his situation, had determined to die game. His great shaggy head, filled with burrs, was lowered to the ground as he confronted his would-be executioners; his tongue, black and parched, lolled out of his mouth, and he gave utterance at intervals to a suppressed roar.

The wolves were sitting on their haunches in a semicircle immediately in front of the tortured beast, and every time that the fear-stricken buffalo gave vent to his hoarsely modulated groan, the wolves howled in concert in most mournful cadence.

After contemplating his antagonists for a few moments, the bull made a dash at the nearest wolf, tumbling him howling over the silent prairie; but while this diversion was going on in front, the remainder of the pack started for his hind legs to hamstring him. Upon this the poor beast turned to the point of attack, only to receive a repetition of it in the same vulnerable place by the wolves, who had as quickly turned also and fastened themselves on his heels again. His hind quarters now streamed with blood, and he began to show signs of great physical weakness. He did not dare to lie down; that•would have been instantly fatal. By this time he had killed three of the wolves, or so maimed them that they were entirely out of the fight.

At this juncture the suffering animal was mercifully shot, and the wolves allowed to batten on his thin and tough carcass.

JUDGE LYNCH'S COURT AT WHOOPING HOLLOW.

WHOOPING HOLLOW is the uneuphonious name of a mining camp in the very heart of the Taos Range — or rather, *was*, for it has been expunged from the map these twenty-five years, and but few of the present generation in New Mexico are aware that such a place ever existed. It was almost inaccessible, so awfully abrupt and broken were the bare granite ridges surrounding it, out of which the circumscribed valley in which the town lay seemed to have been literally scooped when the rocks were plastic — Titanic hands holding the

192

scraper, and the lightning the propelling power.
How the place received its strange appellation
was a mystery even to the majority of the miners
who worked there for nearly five years with picks,
shovels, long-toms, sluices, and other appliances
for extracting the ore from the refractory rock.
The quantity of the precious metals shipped during that period made the camp famous, and resulted in building up a town of rude shanties and
dugouts which at the height of its prosperity
numbered over twelve hundred souls. But you
cannot find Whooping Hollow on any modern
map, for it played out in less than six years from
the date of the discovery of gold there; though
several fortunes were mined in that time, and
made by traffic the specialty of which was bad
whisky.

There was a legend current in the early days of
the valley's occupancy, that was honestly believed
in, which affirmed that the first party of pros-
pectors, consisting of four or five men, all Tennesseeans, who entered the great cañon in their
search, were rewarded well for their pains, finding
plenty of water, game, fuel, together with other
necessaries in the prosecution of their vocation —
a beautiful place for their camp, lots of silver,
and gold in paying quantities — were scared out

—13

of the gulch (to which they never returned) by
an unearthly screeching, seemingly emanating
from a human throat. Its ghostly owner, they
declared, visited their camp every night about 11
o'clock, and on the top of a timbered knoll, where
they could plainly see it as the moonlight sifted
through the scattered piñons and dwarfed cedars,
took its stand, setting up its blood-curdling cries,
which it continued with short intervals of cessa-
tion, until daybreak. Those men, it was alleged,
were a very ignorant and superstitious set, who,
after three nights of their weird experience, could
bear it no longer, and were absolutely driven away
through fright.

Of course they told others of their rich strike,
not forgetting to mention the "hant" of the
place, as they called it; but these others, old
mountaineers, not fearing any disturbance from
the moonlight specter, went there, established
their camp—to which hundreds soon flocked—
calling it Whooping Hollow, in derision of the
tale told by the alarmed Tennesseeans; which
name it retained during its whole existence, and
was known and recognized by that as a postoffice
on the mail records in Washington.

In all probability what the men really heard
was the mottled or American screech-owl, which

makes a plaintive noise, and a peculiar sound
during part of its mournful notes, like the chat-
tering of teeth, keeping up its alternating whooping and moaning all night. It loves to perch on
some blasted tree in the moonlight, and the dis-
embodied form seen by the superstitious miners
must have been a shattered and denuded piñon,
on which the nocturnal bird sat, that, escaping
their vision in the daytime, was exaggerated by
their frightened eyes at night into the " hant " of
the place!—But this is not a ghost story, and the
reader will pardon the digression.

The region in which Whooping Hollow was situated is the roughest, and, to employ a mining
phrase, the " lumpiest " portion of the whole Taos
range. It is a deep gulch in the strictest interpretation of the word, formed by two lofty divides,
whose crests tower skyward from their bases more
than 8,000 feet, which themselves are over 5,000
feet above the Atlantic's level, and the distance
across the narrow valley at its widest part scarcely
three-quarters of a mile. The angle of the slope
of the two opposing mountains is a little less than
85 degrees, making their sides, as may be inferred,
very precipitous.

The town's era of prosperity was long before the
days of railroads in that portion of the continent,

and such feats of engineering as have been accomplished since in the way of "hog-backs," loops and tunnels were not dreamed of as among the possibilities of mountain travel. Nor was there even a wagon-road to Whooping Hollow. Such a thing would have been regarded equally as difficult and expensive as the wonderful achievement of the Atchison, Topeka & Santa Fé in climbing the Raton Range a dozen years later. Everything was "packed" into the place on muleback, at a minimum cost of twenty-five cents a pound, whether the simplest necessaries of life or a sawmill, and the zig-zag trail the sure-footed beasts were compelled to travel up and down the fearful slopes of the great divides to get in and out of the rocky streets of the narrow town, made one dizzy to look at.

The rude collection of shanties, through courtesy called the town of Whooping Hollow, was built on one side of a little creek which ran at a fearful rate in the bottom of the gulch, whose waters, boiling and foaming, like all mountain streams, rushed over and around the immense bowlders with which its narrow bed was choked; while on the opposite side, immediately facing the principal street, extending for miles both ways, on the hill, the mining claims were located.

The houses were in most instances mere shells, constructed of rough slabs; while a few were of hewn logs, presenting a relatively neat appearance. The roofs of all, however, were flat, and covered with earth; they rose one above the other like a flight of stairs, so that one could easily step out of his door upon the top of his neighbor's dwelling below, so precipitous was the side of the mountain on which the place was of necessity laid out. The town consisted of four streets — one devoted entirely to business, the other three to residences only. There were five stores, whose stock was of that character known throughout the West and in the mountains as "general." That is, their proprietors almost literally kept everything, from a toothpick to a steam engine, or from a shoestring to a silk dress. The place boasted also of twelve banks — of deposit only — faro and monte; for the unfortunate individual who once laid his money on the green-cloth tables of these institutions rarely saw any of it again: it was permanently invested! Of saloons, too, Whooping Hollow had its full complement — I think there were thirty at one time; and their owners were not obliged to contribute anything to the support of the town, for as to municipal expenses, there were none. Yet the discipline of

the place was fair, to say the least: the ratio of
violent deaths to the number of inhabitants was
not nearly as great as in any of the Eastern cities;
and as to thieving or burglary, such crimes were
as rare as a church service—which Whooping
Hollow never had during the whole period of its
existence. Of course such a unique condition of
morality is easily accounted for. "Judge Lynch's"
court was the only tribunal for the trial of offenses
against the peace and dignity of the town, and
from its decisions there was no appeal. Besides,
society there was so constituted that it could condone a murder if there existed the slightest shadow
of extenuating circumstances, but it would never
forgive the unlawful appropriation of another's
goods, particularly of horses; horse-stealing being the unpardonable sin, as it is generally on
the frontier, the prompt remedy for which was
"a short shrift and a long rope."

Notwithstanding the fact that perhaps there
were hundreds of men in Whooping Hollow to
whose ears the shrill whistle of a bullet would
sound sweeter than the soft notes of a flute, still
their general good-nature, when sober, and princi-
ple of "honor among thieves," kept them within
bounds. Occasionally—very naturally, too—
there were desperate fights over the gambling-

tables in the hells which abounded in Whooping
Hollow, and frequently an outrageously obstrep-
erous individual, full of "bug-juice," as the vile
whisky dispensed in the saloons was called, would
get a hole drilled into him by a No. 44 revolver-
ball, or his vitals carved with an eleven-inch
bowie. But arrests were rarely made in quarrels
of that character, because extenuating circumstances generally existed. Often, under the excellent care of the skillful doctor—a former army
surgeon, who had established himself there—the
belligerents would recover from their fearful encounter, but oftener took up their last "claim"
of six-feet-by-two in "The Bone Orchard," as the
cemetery on the timbered knoll (where it was
alleged the "hant" was originally seen) had been
dubbed by the citizens of Whooping Hollow.

The average miner (and the miners' claims
radiated from the place in all directions at vary-
ing distances, some as far as thirty miles) would
come into town once a week at least, generally
Sunday, and if he had been fortunate in his diggings would make a break for the first gaming-
table in his way. If he by any chance won he
would "make the rounds," which in local par-
lance meant stopping at every saloon to treat the
crowd of thirsty bummers always present on such

occasions, and sometimes provoking a quarrel
with the first man who got in his way. But if
losing, the rule generally, he went drunk and
sulky back to his claim, consoling himself with
the hope of better luck next time. And so the
lives of the majority were passed. Not a few died
"with their boots on" in some drunken row with
their friends, to whom they had offered a real or
fancied insult.

As in all mining-camps at the period of Whooping Hollow's boom, a most heterogeneous crowd
composed its residents and transient occupiers.
In its rough but busy streets you met all shades
and nationalities. The tall, plodding Yankee,
fresh from the hills of New England, green as a
gourd, but with sufficient gall to extricate himself
from any little difficulty he might stumble into;
the active, restless Texan; the jauntily dressed
commercial traveler, with his samples of bad
whisky and worse cigars; the swarthy Mexican,
with his broad sombrero, scarlet sash, and irre-
pressible *cigarito;* that darker specimen of the
genus homo, the negro; and, last of all, the
"heathen Chinee." Nearly every State had its
dozens of representatives in the motley group of
individuals who had come to seek their fortunes
in this new El Dorado. It was a grand place to

study character; to learn how all the finer attributes of man may be completely crushed out of
his nature by years of adversity, and how, under
the same circumstances in others, all that is noble
and pure predominates, no matter how hellish
or pestilential, morally, may have been their
surroundings.

The principal store of the town was owned and
conducted by Jemuel Knaggs, a man of reputable
character, an old plainsman and mountaineer, full
of enterprise and grit, the acknowledged "leading
citizen" of Whooping Hollow. In every community, whether the most enlightened or barbarous, there is always to be found some individual
who, by his force of character and other inherent
attributes, becomes foremost in all that concerns
the welfare and prosperity of the people who compose it, and this was the rôle that Jemuel Knaggs
played in the rough mining-camp of Whooping
Hollow. He was a veteran miner, too, of Cali-
fornia in '49; Fraser river, in British Columbia,
in '58; and Pike's Peak in '59. But having
amassed several thousand dollars during his erratic wanderings, in 1859 he abandoned the pick
and shovel for the more pleasant occupation of
keeping a general miners' store, whose necessities
none knew better than he. So he opened up in

Whooping Hollow in the days of its incipiency. He was a man about fifty years old, rather slender than otherwise, but there was something in his air and features which distinguished him from common men. The expression of his countenance was keen and daring; his forehead was high, and his lips thin and compressed, indicating great determination of will. One would not have hesitated to confide in his honor or courage, but would have been extremely reluctant to provoke his hostility. He always wore a dark-blue navy shirt, to the collar of which was attached a curious button. Around his waist was tightly buckled a broad leather belt, in which a formidable looking bowie-knife was stuck; to be used, as is usual with all frontiersmen, for various purposes indifferently — to kill a man, cut food, pick his teeth, or for whittling when he had nothing else to do.

Matters progressed very smoothly in Whooping Hollow for two or three years, under the watchful care of Knaggs and a few others of like sterling character, who will be hurriedly described as they appear in this sketch. But at the end of that period a pall suddenly fell on the place. Men would leave for a visit to some neighboring camp or on a hunting expedition, and never be heard of again. Sometimes it would be one of the best citizens who would disappear all at once; the number of instances of this character in one year aggregating twenty. At last the whole town became aroused, and suspicions of foul play in the matter entered their heretofore apparently too lethargic brains. No one felt safe, and when, to "cap the climax" as it were, Jemuel Knaggs was declared "missing," an investigation was immediately but secretly instituted.

It then developed that with one or two exceptions all of those who had disappeared had left Whooping Hollow for Sandy Bar, the nearest mining-camp, sixty miles distant, and to which there was only one possible trail over the divide. That the parties had been murdered was now conceded; but upon whom could suspicion rest? and where on the lonely route were the damnable, deeds committed? These were the questions discussed one evening by half a dozen prominent men of Whooping Hollow, who had secretly met in a room about a week after Jemuel Knaggs failed to return at the appointed time. He was last seen on the day of his departure from town by some reputable miners, who had met and conversed with him on the trail to Sandy Bar, not more than twelve miles from his home. He had never arrived at Sandy Bar, however; that fact was ascertained to a certainty through diligent inquiry there. It was only a small camp of less than three hundred people, and he was as well known there as in Whooping Hollow.

About half-way between Whooping Hollow and Sandy Bar there was a narrow, rocky valley, known as Willow Springs Gulch; abandoned long ago as a mining region, the ore in that vicinity having consisted of a series of small "pockets" only, which were naturally exhausted in less than six months from the date of their discovery, and that was more than two years before operations had begun in Whooping Hollow. But the place was still famous for its pure water, which gushed out of the indurated wall of a small cañon in a stream as large as a man's arm — clear, cold and sparkling; the best water to be found in the whole sixty miles' ride. The entrance to the rocky cañon was almost concealed by a dense growth of mountain willows; hence the name. But the beautiful spring was the only redeeming feature in the otherwise barren and desolate landscape. Near this lonely spot stood a small adobe cabin, or rather hut, the only habitation anywhere within twenty miles of the dreary place. Its sole occupant was a miner, ostensibly, who

pretended to own a claim near Sandy Bar, but it-
was alleged that no one ever saw him work it;
yet he always apparently had sufficient money
to supply his wants, ever paying gold for his
purchases. He was a tall, angular, villainous-
looking specimen of humanity; rough, illiterate,
dialectic in his talk, but possessing the physique
of a giant, as courageous as a she-grizzly with
cubs, a dead shot with the revolver, and withal
believed by every one to be a desperado in the
most rigid acceptation of the term. Viewed su-
perficially—for nobody at Whooping Hollow or
Sandy Bar knew anything about his antecedents
—he was apparently without one redeeming quality, except that he was kind to his dog, a mangy,
spotted, wicked - looking yellow cur, with only
one eye, and tailless—fit companion for such a
surly-disposed master. This strangely mysterious
being, with whom no one had any more intercourse than was absolutely necessary, and that
confined to the limited conversation required
when he entered stores to make purchases, lived
a supremely isolated sort of an existence, for he
was as carefully avoided by every one as were the
rattlesnakes that infested the rocky arroyos of
the bald bleak hills where his hut was located.
Upon him, then, black suspicion naturally at-

once fell — so prone is human nature to be guided
by visible forms; though there was not an inkling
of proof, either circumstantial or direct, upon
which to base this man's guilt.

Fortunately, they who were quietly investigat-
ing the cause of the disappearance of Jemuel
Knaggs were men of excellent judgment; cool,
calm and deliberate in their proceedings, but terribly in earnest. They had received their education in the great "school of the world": they
knew that suspicions were not facts; that appear-
ances are too often deceiving; and they were
nonplussed because convincing proof was not
forthcoming to convict the only man upon whom
a shadow of probable guilt could fall.

This strange creature, about whom nobody
knew anything, was called, whenever reference to
him became necessary (often now, for he was in
everyone's thought a murderer), "Willow Gulch
Jack," because his real name was not ever known
—adopting the Indian's method of nomenclature
and associating him with his locality. It may
readily be inferred that it was only his villainous
aspect and isolated life that brought this whole-
sale condemnation upon him, for he had never
been guilty of any disreputable act that the people could discover, and now they left no stone

unturned to find something against him; but they avoided and suspected him as a sheep-raiser does a strange cur in his neighborhood. Consequently a system of espionage was inaugurated on his movements, but nothing, as yet, had been discovered to cast a shadow on his every-day life. He knew that he was suspected and watched; so, for some special reason which had not yet been made clear to the people of Whooping Hollow, he was now almost constantly absent from home, passing his time on the trail between his cabin and the top of the divide above the town, always accompanied by the one-eyed, tailless dog, his constant companion. His enemies were aware of his perambulations, but could not divine the cause, and the mystery connected with his isolated life seemed to them more impenetrable than ever. Of course they did not hound his every footstep, because, as they reasoned, that would give him no opportunity to commit himself; they merely adopted such precautionary measures as would prevent his escape from the country, and that would permit them to arrest him at any time they wanted to if he attempted to leave, or whenever they had gathered sufficient proof to convict him, which as yet seemed as remote as ever — flattering themselves all the while that he was unconscious of their intentions.

One day, about two weeks after the investigation of the cause of the disappearance of Jemuel Knaggs had been fairly inaugurated, this Willow Gulch Jack, as I shall have to call him in the absence of the knowledge of his real name, rode quietly into Whooping Hollow, dismounted, tied his mule to a stump in front of Tom Bradford's log cabin, walked up to the door, gave it a heavy kick, and waited until it was opened — his cur, at a word from his master, lying down close to the mule.

Tom Bradford was a veteran miner, one of the best citizens Whooping Hollow possessed, whose opinions on important matters were generally regarded as conclusive — such faith the curiously assorted people of the town placed in his excellent judgment, which fact Jack was fully aware of. Bradford himself came out on the porch in response to Jack's tremendous knock, but when he saw who his visitor was, a shade of evident displeasure passed over his countenance — for he too, although he knew that not a scintilla of proof had been forthcoming after all these days of investigation, believed in this man's guilt. Tom Bradford regarded Jack intently for a moment, as if wondering what to say or do, so astonished was he at his presence; but Jack broke the painful silence in a few words:

"I say, Tom Bradford," (nobody was "mis-
tered" out there in those days,) "I hev kim ter
talk ter ye. I knows this hyar's onexpected, but
I don't keer, an' w'at I hev ter tell I wants ter tell
ye whar no one kin har we-uns. Hev yer sich a
place whar we-uns kin converse ondisturbed?"

Bradford eyed Jack closely for a few seconds —
not that he had any fear of the man, villainous
as he looked, and giant that he was — then told
him to follow as he led the way through the cabin
door. They passed out of one room into another
at the rear (there were only two apartments in
the building), where he pushed a dilapidated
rush-bottomed chair toward Jack, himself taking
another, and, throwing his feet upon a rickety
table, the only other article of furniture in the
rude log den, he pulled his pipe out of his pocket,
filled it, lighted it, and handed another to Jack
with the tobacco from a box nailed against the
wall within easy reach. He gave a few vigorous
pulls at his own, emitting a cloud of smoke that
almost enveloped him, then, fixing his eyes on his
unwelcome visitor, said:

"Now then, I'm ready to hear what you have
got to communicate."

"Tom Bradford," began Jack upon this invitation, "I knows thet I hev been 'spected of these
— 14

hyar murders w'at hev tuk place; an' I knows thet
I hev been hounded an' watched, which you-uns
hed no idee I knowed; but ye knows, Tom Bradford, thar haint er shadder kin be proved agin
me."

"I am aware of that," said Bradford, hurriedly;
"and although you are and have been the only
man in the mines suspected, we folks here are
determined that no innocent person shall suffer
upon mere suspicion and under the excitement
of the moment; we are also determined that no
guilty party—or parties, if there should be more
than one person implicated—shall escape the
swift, summary punishment the hellish acts de-
serve. We have no organized courts here, but
organize them as we need them ourselves. No
mere technicality will save a rascal either, as it
does sometimes in what are called civilized com-
munities."

"Tom Bradford," continued Jack, "you nor
no one else hez ever seen me a-loafin' roun' saloons; nor gamblin'-hells; an' no one hain't never
seen me drunk nuther—hev they? I knows my
looks is agin me; but looks hain't nothin', nor
no judge ter go by. I hain't no harnsome man—
never sot any claim ter sich. I oncet tuk ther
prize fer grinnin' through a hoss-collar, at er

county fair way back in old Kaintuk, w'en I war young."

At this admission a change that was evidently intended for a smile suddenly crept over Jack's face as he opened his ponderous jaws; but the effect made his cavernous mouth, which literally stretched from ear to ear, look as if it had been made by a broadax at a blow.

"Waal," he continued, as the paroxysm caused by the remembrance of his youth passed off, "I hev been doin' some detective work myself; an' w'at I hev diskivered is w'at hez brung me hyar ter talk ter ye 'bout. It war all a accident, though; an' ef it hed n't 'a' been fer thet thar ornery dorg o' mine, I would n't er foun' out nothin'. You-uns 'll all be surprised ez I wuz, w'en ye kim ter larn who ther murd'rer for sartin is. In ther fust place, I knowed them folkses ez war missin' never got pas' my cabin "——

Bradford looked Jack suddenly in the eye, as if to catch the true meaning of his last assertion; but Jack, seeing that he was misunderstood, became a little heated, and in a most emphatic manner said:

"Never reached thar, Tom Bradford, ez I wants ye ter onderstand! Now I wants yer ter tell me," he continued, getting more excited, "how.many cabins—whar folkses lives, I means; 'course thar's lots o' 'bandoned ones—'twixt Whoopin' Holler an' mine?"

"Well," replied Bradford, in response to Jack's interrogatory, "there are but two—Cal. Jones's and Ike Podgett's. Why?"

"Don't yer see, Tom Bradford, ef them ez is missin' never got ter my cabin, they never got by one o' them t'others?"

"What do you mean?" asked Bradford, looking up excitedly into Jack's face.

"I means jes' w'at I says," replied Jack, gazing as earnestly now into Bradford's. "Ef er man leaves Whoopin' Holler fer Sandy Bar, he kain't git offen ther trail, kin he? Thar hain't but one trail, is thar? An' ef he don't kim back, an' don't go ahead, he mus' 'a' stopped somewhar 'twixt ther two places, mus'n't he? An' ef he haint heerd of fer a long while, he mus' hev stopped fer good, eh? Now do yer understan', Tom Bradford?" and Jack emphasized his remarks by bringing down his huge fist like a sledge-hammer on top of the rickety old table right in front of Bradford.

Tom Bradford smiled at Jack's earnestness, and looking him squarely in the eyes, said:

"Why, you must be insane, man! Cal. Jones's

cabin is right on the highest point of the divide.
If you were out on my porch, you could see it
from here. You ain't crazy enough to suppose
that a murder could be committed at such an exposed place, and everybody in town not know it
in ten minutes? And as for Ike Podgett—ha!
ha! ha! Ike Podgett! why, man, Ike Podgett is
one of our best citizens; one of the most enter-
prising men in the place; always has plenty of
money; spends it freely, too. To be sure he gam-
bles some, and drinks. Who don't? They are
mighty few—you know that. He don't come to
town very often; stays at home a good deal; but
then, he's got a fine paying claim, and works it
for all there is in it; at least that is what he tells
all of us here in town. Ike Podgett—ha! ha!
ha! That's a good one, I swear!"

Jack's eyes snapped as Bradford laughed in his
face. He was getting mad at the manner in which
his statements were being received; he grew very
red, and blurted out:

"Ike Podgett hain't home now, is he?"

"No," answered Bradford; "he's gone bear-
hunting with a lot of the boys; been gone several
days; won't be back for a week yet; they were
going as far as the Spanish Peaks."

"His'n is er mighty lonesome place, hain't it?"
queried Jack.

"Yes," answered Bradford, "a mighty lone-some place. I don't see how he can live there— such a rocky, dark cañon—hardly a ray of sun-light enters there until late in the afternoon. But he says he loves solitude, and don't like neighbors too near"—

"I'm his closest, I reckon," interrupted Jack again.

"I believe you are," replied Bradford.

"He's married, though, hain't he, to a Spanish woman?—on'y a child, 'pears ter me; I've seed her oncet or twicet."

"He's got a woman out there with him—don't know whether she's his wife or mistress. We folks here don't bother our heads about such mat-ters; it's none of our business; she's Mexican, though," answered Bradford. "But why," con-tinued he, impatient and disgusted with the inter-view's length, "why do you ask these ridiculous questions? I have no time to waste!" He then petulantly rose, knocked the ashes out of his pipe, evidently tired, and determined to end the matter right there and get rid of his annoying visitor.

"'Cause, Tom Bradford," slowly and solemnly replied Jack, at the same time getting up from his chair, too; and putting his mouth close to Brad-ford's ear, he hoarsely whispered:

" 'Cause Ike Podgett is the murderer of Jemnel Knaggs, anyhow, an' w'y not o' all the t'others ez is missin' ? "

" My God, man ! what do you mean ?" excitedly asked Tom Bradford, suddenly wheeling around and placing both of his hands on Jack's shoulders.

" Tom Bradford, I mean 'zac'ly w'at I kin prove ; an' ter tell this hyar is w'at hez brung me ter this hyar cabin."

" Hold on ! " cried Bradford, violently agitated ; "you must prove it, must tell all you know; but in the presence of others. Wait—sit down here —I 'll be back directly, and bring some one with me. Wait ! " and Bradford rushed out into the street in a terrible state of excitement.

He returned in less than twenty minutes in company with a short, thick-set, grizzly veteran miner, a man about sixty years of age. This was old man Bartlett—better known, however, and generally accosted as " Judge," because he had so frequently presided over the locally instituted courts in the diggings everywhere he had been during his long career in the mountains and on the Plains. He was regarded by everybody as the most level-headed, honest and discreet man in the whole Range. In fact, that had been his reputation wherever he had traveled, following him

in all his erratic wanderings since his advent in
the Far West, forty years before he turned up in
Whooping Hollow. He had "whacked bulls" on
the old Santa Fé trail; had lived for months on
hardtack and bacon in the mountains of Califor-
nia; had nearly starved to death on the sage-bush
plains of Nevada; had been captured by Apaches
in Arizona, but was rescued by a detachment of
United States dragoons just in time to escape the
torture of the stake, the fires for which were already lighted; and years before all these strange
experiences, had "filibustered" with Walker in
Nicaragua. Altogether, he had seen as eventful
a life as ever fell to the fortune of one man.

When the two men entered the little barren log
room where Jack was, they found him sitting at
its only window, his number twelve feet on the
broad sill, pulling vigorously at the clay pipe that
Bradford in his rough hospitality had originally
provided him with, blowing great rings of smoke
out of his huge mouth as he sat there as imper-
turbable as a rock. He greeted Bartlett with a
short "Howdy, Jedge," and then resumed his
pipe, waiting for him or Bradford to open the
conversation.

Old Sam pulled an enormous plug of navy tobacco from his hip pocket, tore off a liberal por-

tion with his teeth, rolled the immense quid over
in his mouth several times, and then, looking
earnestly at Jack as if to measure him in his
mind, said:

"Jack, Bradford's been telling me some mighty
queer stories. Ike Podgett a murderer? I don't
believe a word of it. He," jerking his thumb
toward Bradford, "wanted me to come over and
hear your statement, which I agreed to; but I tell
you beforehand, the proofs will have to be clear
as Holy Writ to convince me that Ike Podgett
knows what has become of Jemuel Knaggs any
more than me and Tom here does."

"The Judge" was not always a rigid follower
of the rules laid down by Lindley Murray in the
construction of his sentences, therefore frequently
got the cases of his pronouns mixed, although he
was a college graduate; but he generally talked
fairly correctly.

"Let's hear your story," continued he; "tell
us what you know, and how you know, as you
have asserted to Bradford that Ike Podgett killed
Jemuel Knaggs."

"Waal," commenced Jack, leaving his place at
the window, rising to his full height, stretching
out his long arms, giving a tremendous yawn as
he did so; then moving his chair to the end of

the table between the two men, who had seated
themselves on opposite sides, their feet of course
on top, where, resting his elbows on it, his immense paws supporting his, shaggy head, Jack
looked his interlocutor squarely in the eyes, and
continued:

"Waal, yer knows, sence I war satisfied that I
war a-bein' watched an' hounded an' 'spected by
you-uns hyar in Whoopin' Holler, I 'lowed ter
myself thet I would do a leetle *detective* work on
my own 'count — ez I hev told Bradford hyar.
So I gits onto my mule, tuks Jupe — thet's thet
thar yaller, no-'count, ornery dorg o' mine — an'
we jes' nat'rally comminces ter prowl thet thar
trail from t'other side o' Ike Podgett's 'twixt thar
an' ther Holler, fer more'n er week. But we-uns
didn't see nothin' 'spicious till day afore yister-
day, 'long in ther shank o' ther evenin'. Then I
war ridin' by Podgett's place — Jupe hed run
'way 'head o' me — I war goin' toler'ble slow an'
thinkin' powerful; an' w'en I got clos't ter ther
cabin, I seed thet thar fool dorg o' mine er dig-
gin' an' er pawin' et suthin' he hed unyearthed.
Ther no-'count cuss is always hungry an' always
huntin' fer suthin ter eat. Then ez I obsarved
thar warn't no one ter home, I gits down offen my
mule, hitches him, an' lights out fer ther r'ar o'

ther cabin whar ther dorg war, ter see w'at he
war so consarned 'bout; an' w'en I reached thar,
gentlemin, et war a human leg and foot. An'
stoopin' down, I picked this hyar outen ther dirt
ther dorg hed pawed up! "

Getting up from his seat as he said this, Jack
pulled out of the breast-pocket of his flannel shirt
a little mass of iron pyrites, an octahedrite in
shape — a rare form of that common combination
of iron and sulphur — which was drilled onto a
plate of gold, making it a perfect but unique
collar-button.

"Great God!" exclaimed Bartlett and Bradford simultaneously, as they both jumped up excitedly at the sight of the trinket Jack held in
his hand.

Tom Bradford gave vent to his feelings first.
Slapping his fist on the table, and then pointing
his finger at Jack, who stood as calm as a statue,
said vehemently:

" Judge Bartlett, either this man's story is true,
or he is the murderer himself! "

"Great God!" reiterated Bartlett, putting his
hand to his head in his evident bewilderment;
" Bradford — I don't know — I 'm completely
dumbfounded! Everybody in the mines knows
that collar-button. There 's not another one like

it in the mountains. Knaggs always wore it at
the neck of his flannel shirt. He 's told me many
a time that he 'd refused $50 for it. This matter
must be thoroughly investigated."   ·

He then reached for the button, which Jack
promptly handed to him, and which he examined
carefully for a few moments in silence, sitting
down for that purpose. Then turning suddenly
to Jack, who—now conscious that he had at least
caused Bradford and Bartlett to believe that he
might be innocent, and that his story might be
true—had resumed his seat, and was coolly fill-
ing his pipe again, the old Judge asked him:

"Jack, did you leave the leg and foot where
the dog found it, or what did you do with it?"

"I left it thar," replied Jack, but I kivered it
up agin; an' I stomped ther groun' down 'roun'
it so ez it looked like it hed n't been tech'd. Then
I went ter my cabin; then I kim hyar ter Bradford's. Ther on'y thing I brung 'way war thet
button, an' fer which I 'll thank yer ter gin me
ag'in. I wants to keep it er while yit!"

Bartlett hesitated a moment, rolling over in
his fingers the mute evidence of a crime committed; looked at Bradford interrogatively, who nod-
ded significantly, and then he handed the curious
object back to Jack.

"Thank ye, gentlemin," said he, as he put it carefully into his pocket again; "I'm et yer sarvice et any time, and so is this hyar button w'en ye wants it; an' I hopes you-ns means ter 'vestigate this hyar matter ter oncet. Ike Podgett's 'way now, an' w'en he kims back it's mebby too late."

Bartlett and Bradford consulted aside in a low tone for a few moments; then walking back to the table where Jack was still sitting, pulling at his pipe, and almost invisible because of the smoke, the old Judge said:

"Jack, this is a strange piece of business, and we are both staggered. Yet we are not unreasonable; we know that nothing is more deceptive than a man's estimate of human nature; it seems mighty hard to come to your way of thinking; but we all may have been most terribly deceived in Ike Podgett. We will examine his premises and investigate the matter to the end. Now we want you to go quietly out to your cabin from here; say nothing to anyone about what you have told us. To-night we will discuss, with some of our best citizens, what is best to be done; and to-morrow meet us at Podgett's. If we arrive there first we will wait right on the trail for you, and take no action before you come; but if you get to

the place before we do, wait for our party. Don't
go near the cabin and don't touch a thing, and
then nobody can raise any suspicions of a job,
which some of Podgett's friends might accuse you
of. We will try to be there by eleven o'clock,
and that will allow you ample time to reach there
as soon as that hour too.''

The old Judge having finished his instructions
and warnings, the three men went out of the
cabin and separated. Jack mounted his mule,
whistled to Jupe, and rode slowly up the steep
divide into the hills, where he was soon lost to
sight. Bartlett and Bradford walked down to
the main street, their feelings wonderfully affected, and entered the little building that did
duty as the postoffice for Whooping Hollow and
surrounding mining-camps, to look up the proper
persons with whom to consult concerning the terrible revelations of a few moments before.

That evening just after the candles were lighted,
Judge Bartlett, Tom Bradford, Doctor Chase, and
Issachar Noe, the last of whom was postmaster,
met in the little rectangular space behind the
rude rack of letter-boxes in Noe's store, to formu-
late plans for their trip on the morrow to Ike
Podgett's cabin, the bloody story concerning it
having been imparted to Noe and the Doctor when

Bartlett and Bradford came down-town that afternoon, immediately after their interview with Jack.

A little after daylight next morning the four
prominent citizens of Whooping Hollow who had
secretly met at the postoffice the previous evening
were well on the trail to Podgett's. They had
only twenty-three miles to go, but the zigzag
up to the crest of the divide was so rocky, rough
and precipitous that they were compelled to
"wind" their horses every few rods; consequently the trip was so fatiguing to both men
and animals that they did not arrive there until
nearly noon.

Podgett's cabin, one of the better class, roomy,
and adorned with a veranda, was situated in the
most God-forsaken looking region imaginable.
There was not a tree, bush, or any vegetation, not
even a cactus, in sight. It was hidden among
great water-worn columns of lava, which so completely enveloped it in their ominous shadows that
only late in the afternoon the sun's lingering rays,
low down in the west, entered the gloomy cañon
in which the isolated cabin was located.

"God in Israel!" said Issachar Noe — a favorite expression of his when excited —"how can a
man content himself in such a spot as this? I
would n't live here for a hundred dollars an hour,"

he continued, as he surveyed the dismal surroundings of the barren and repulsive place.

"Some men love solitude," said the Doctor, as
if in response to Noe's comments. "I know many
natures among my acquaintances in the East who
could be perfectly happy in such a sequestered
spot as this. To them, solitude is the nurse of
enthusiasm, and "—

"Great Cæsar!" interrupted Tom Bradford,
destroying at once the thread of the Doctor's philosophy. "See those wolves!" at the same moment pointing with his "quirt" to half a dozen
or more of that large gray mountain species that
were scampering over the angular lava bowlders
up the cañon in the rear of the cabin. These animals had not before been observed, because the
party from town had seated themselves on the
trail immediately in front of the hut, upon their
arrival at the place. They had not ventured any
nearer, in accordance with the agreement made at
the conference held in Tom Bradford's room that
neither the party nor Jack was to investigate
alone, but together.

·In a few moments the cause of the wolves' hasty
retreat made its appearance in the shape of the
one-eyed tailless dog Jupe, slowly shambling
around a curve in the trail, closely followed by

the gaunt, angular figure of Jack, seated on his
mule. As he approached, the party from Whooping Hollow, who were reclining on the rocks scattered on the trail, rose, while Jack, dismounting,
hitched his animal to a bowlder, and saluting all
with a "Howdy, gents," he joined them. Then
without further talk at that moment, they proceeded to the rear of Ike Podgett's cabin, piloted
by Jack. They soon arrived at the spot he had
told Bradford and Bartlett of, but the moment he
cast his eyes on the place he exclaimed:

"Great heavens! ther wolves hev been hyar!"

The earth was torn up, and lying on the edge of
the shallow grave, sure enough, were a human leg
and foot — the same described by Jack, which he
had reinterred, but which the wolves had again
dragged out of the hole.

"Well, I'm ——!" ejaculated old Sam Bartlett,
as he contemplated the horrid spectacle, and he
vigorously mopped his bald head—out of which
the perspiration now oozed in great beads—with
an enormous red bandana.

"There's no question about that leg and foot,"
said the Doctor, as he stooped and picked up the
ghastly objects to examine them more closely.
"They're human—no getting over that, but
whether they belonged to Jemuel Knaggs, of

—15

course I can't say." Pulling them out of the soft
dirt, he found clinging to the end of the femur a
piece of cloth of some kind, which the instant
Tom Bradford saw he took in his hands, held it
up, and exclaimed:

"Well, this is the last straw that breaks the
camel's back for me!" All could see that it was
the fragment of a blue flannel shirt, its broad
collar, with the buttonhole, torn apart.

"A piece of Jemuel Knagg's shirt, or I'm a
liar," solemnly said Issachar Noe, as he gazed on
the bit of telltale garment. "He always wore
that kind," continued Noe. "I sent to St. Louis
for them myself for him; that is a part of one of
them."

The astounded party, upon this confirmation of
Podgett's guilt, looked at each other in silence for
a few seconds, when Bartlett, breaking the awful
stillness, said:

"Gentlemen, I've seen enough here! Let's go
and examine the cabin — which we've got a right
to do now, as law-abiding citizens, after such
damnable revelations outside of it!"

On entering the cabin, effected by the colossal
Jack making a sort of a side-lurch against the
door, which immediately flew off its hinges at his
first essay, they discovered in the corner of the

room used as a kitchen a spot where the dirt floor seemed to yield a little to the pressure of their feet as they walked over it, appearing as if it had been disturbed quite recently. Searching for some implement with which to examine the suspicious corner more closely, they at last found a spade hanging on a peg in the wall of another apartment, evidently the sleeping-room. Here and there were evidences of a woman's occupancy. Under the bed a No. 1 pair of shoes tantalizingly obtruded. On the bed itself a corset was lying, where it had apparently been hastily thrown off by its petite owner; and suspended from some hooks in the logs forming the side of the building were several skirts and other portions of female apparel. For a moment, but only for a moment, these things, so rare in the mining-camps of that period, nearly diverted from their mission the stern and honest men who had entered there, so sweetly suggestive were the articles of mother, sister, or perhaps wife, so far away, and bright visions crowded thick upon their brains. It was soon dispelled, however, as the realization of the actual present forced itself upon them; so, taking down the spade from its place, they returned to the kitchen, and Jack, who had volunteered, commenced to dig.

He had not excavated to a depth of more than
two feet when he unearthed the mutilated fragments of another human body! Hereupon he
rested from his labor for a moment; then stooped
down and pulled something out of the hole, his
hands trembling violently as he laid the object
on the floor, and exclaiming as he rose up:

"This hyar gits me, by ——!"

Every one was now almost uncontrollably excited, and if Podgett had at that instant entered
his own door he would have been annihilated by
the infuriated men without a chance to explain,
for just as Jack gave vent to his words he had
lifted out of the hole a head, to which was still
attached a long red beard. He recognized it at
once, and that fact was the cause of his excitement.

"God in Israel!" said Issachar Noe vehemently, as he got down on his knees to view
the ghastly object more closely. "That's Tom
Jackson's head, and he's only been missing about
two months!"

"That's so," solemnly replied old Sam Bartlett. "That's poor Tom's beard, sure enough!"

For more than three hours the now determined
men worked inside and outside the cabin that
they now knew had such a bloody record. At

the end of that time, when they ceased their horrid labor from sheer exhaustion, they had discovered the remains of twelve human bodies, among which was that of a baby's, which sorely puzzled them to account for. Many of the remains, where the head was not too much decayed, they recognized as once citizens of Whooping Hollow who had ridden out from it never to return.

Charred fragments of skeletons, too, were found hidden in holes in the rocks, and it was reasonably supposed that many other victims than those whose bones they had brought to light must have been murdered by the demon Podgett, and their bodies left in the mountains just where he had killed them, to be devoured by the wolves.

Putting portions of several remains in a sack, including the ghastly head of Tom Jackson, they induced Jack — towards whom their manner had entirely changed — to pack the repulsive-looking burden on the back of his mule, and they all returned to town.

The result of their horrible experience was disclosed to several of the most reputable people of the place, who that same evening met with them in the postoffice, in "secret session," to devise plans for Podgett's arrest before he had an opportunity to revisit his cabin. It was conceded that he would come to town first with the hunting party that he had gone out with, which would return in three or four days at farthest, and it was resolved to secure him the moment he made his appearance. To this duty they appointed the now worthy Jack and one Bart Kennedy.

On the afternoon of the fourth day after the meeting, Podgett rode unsuspiciously into town with his companions, and the instant he alighted from his mule found himself locked in Jack's vise-like embrace, who with others had been anxiously watching for his coming. He was at once secured in a little log building, and carefully guarded by two plucky Irish miners who had volunteered their services, for by this time all the law-abiding element of Whooping Hollow had become acquainted with the sickening discoveries at the wretch's cabin.

Podgett thus safely under bolt and bar, a committee was sent over to Sandy Bar to interview his Mexican wife or mistress, whose people lived somewhere in the mountains near there, as it was learned that she had gone home. They found her with her father, a widower, who could speak nothing but Spanish, nor could she speak English at all. But Isaacher Noe, one of the party, understood and conversed in the language like a native; so no interpreter was necessary.

The girl was very young, very pretty, but apparently too youthful for either wife or mother. From her some startling disclosures were elicited. She had witnessed a number of murders at the cabin, but had been afraid to say a word, because Podgett swore that he would kill her if she did. But when he dashed her baby's brains out in the most cruel and atrocious manner, right before her eyes, less than two months ago, she made up her mind that she would expose his bloody life as soon as she could find a safe opportunity. She had run away from him the night he went off hunting, and came to her father's, declaring that she would die before she would go back and consort again with such a monster.

When the committee returned to Whooping Hollow, and had submitted their report, threats were freely and openly made by the exasperated miners that they would take Podgett out of the improvised jail and hang him at once. But better counsel prevailed, and it was finally agreed upon at an open-air meeting held that afternoon that he should have a fair trial, as had always been customary in dealing with criminals since the establishment of the camp. The prisoner would be allowed to select a jury of twelve men himself — but it must be composed of the most reputable

citizens only; a judge should be elected by the
crowd, he to appoint some one competent to
prosecute, and another to defend.

As soon as the preliminaries were agreed to by
the now excited mob, George Burton's general
outfitting store was selected for the court-room,
and the trial set for eight o'clock the same evening. In that community no such thing as the
law's delay was brooked; the citizens of Whooping Hollow believing in swift, stern justice on all
occasions.

Long before the hour appointed for the trial
the crowd began to collect, and by half-past seven
the little room selected was packed to its utmost
capacity. On the outside of the building, compelled to remain in the street, was an indignant,
determined mob, numbering more than three
times as many as were inside, surging backward
and forward, making night hideous with their
yells, blasphemous remarks of impatience, and
muttered threats of "getting even with him,"
"having his heart's blood," etc. Both outside
and inside of that rough log building was gathered as motley and as hard-looking a crowd as
ever got together in the mountains anywhere. It
was a strange admixture of ignorance, manhood,
vice, virtue, and villainy. Some of the truest

men that ever lived stood there; and some were
there, too, as deeply dyed in crime, if the truth
were known about them, as Podgett himself.
Miners, merchants, gamblers and Mexicans were
mixed up promiscuously; but their determined
faces and show of revolvers spoke more eloquently
than language, that "there wasn't going to be
any fooling in the matter."

The dingy-looking room improvised for the purpose of the court was lighted by half a dozen
tallow candles, which shed a dim, sallow haziness
over the piles of bacon, picks, shovels, canned
fruits, and other miners' goods stored there, and
upon the hard-visaged men who had assembled
there to mete out that justice which they believed had been already too long delayed. The
red flames of a blazing fire, made of dry pine-
knots, nearly as combustible as powder, occasionally shot up the throat of the huge chimney
built diagonally across one corner of the room,
whenever a fresh armful was thrown on by the
two boys appointed to that office for the time
being. When the flames had exhausted themselves, and only the embers glowed on the black
hearth, a glimmering and a confused mist seemed
to diffuse itself over the brindled crowd, while
the fitful rays of the unsnuffed candles threw

weird shadows on the whitewashed walls like
ghosts, as if the spirits of the murderer's victims
had come to be phantom witnesses of his agony
and despair.

Old Sam Bartlett, as usual, was chosen judge
without a dissenting voice. A pile of bacon,
packed in gunny-sacks and elevated four or five
feet above the floor, on which Bartlett, with his
legs dangling over the side, sat, constituted the
official bench. The jury, composed of the best
men in town, sat on the right of the judge, on
boxes, nail-kegs, sacks, or anything that came
handy. Ike Podgett, the miserable man for
whom all this strange proceeding was instituted,
crouching on the dirt-begrimed floor between his
two determined guards, rivets his eyes on the
resolute men before him, distracted alternately
by hope and despair; for he now feels the enormity of his guilt, and knows in his cowardly
heart that he deserves death right there, without
the least show of mercy.

Tom Bradford was appointed to prosecute the
case, and a young man — Enoch Green. who had
been graduated from the law school of Yale two
or three years before — was appointed to defend
Podgett. In a few pithy sentences Judge Bartlett
explained the object of the gathering, and re-

viewed the terrible crimes that had been traced to the accused's den in the lonely cañon. He pointed to the ghastly remains and charred fragments of human skeletons piled upon a rude table in front of the jury, which he told them, in wonderfully impressive language, had been dug up, in his own presence, inside of Podgett's cabin and found among the rocks in the vicinity of the accursed place. The indignant old man grew almost eloquent in his recitation of the prisoner's damnable deeds, and a deathlike stillness pervaded the crowd as the words fell hot and earnestly from his lips, only broken now and then by the convulsive click of a revolver as the excited feelings of some pugnacious individual intensified under the judge's burning remarks. But for his admonition of their promise to give the miserable wretch Podgett a trial, in all probability the proceedings would have been ended before Bartlett closed his remarks.

Tom Bradford, in his argument as the legally constituted prosecutor, merely reiterated in a measure what the judge had so forcibly expressed, but he scathed Podgett in a fearful manner, working up a more exasperated feeling, if that were possible, than existed before; and when he had finished his address he called his witnesses.

The Doctor was first to testify; but he confined his evidence to the character of the charred bones, settling beyond the question of possibility that they were human.

Willow Gulch Jack then appeared, and upon him all eyes were concentrated as he related to the jury the simple story. He described accurately, with a dead coal taken from the fireplace, on the top of a cracker-box, the location of the cabin, its surroundings, and the position in which the several bodies were found, particularly that of Jemuel Knaggs, a piece of whose blue shirt and curious collar-button he exhibited, the latter being recognized by nearly every man present. He made a graphic if not artistic sketch with his rude pencil, and its effect upon the jury and spectators was manifested by expressions addressed to Podgett more emphatic than elegant.

Issachar Noe was the next and last witness called for the prosecution. He related in an impressive and convincing manner, as chairman of the committee, the interview with the young wife or mistress of Podgett, which was received by his listeners with that faith in its accuracy comparable to the high character of the man.

Then young Green, the counsel appointed for the defense, though he had not a single particle of evidence to offer, and convinced of the deep villainy of his brutal and inhuman client, felt it incumbent to make an appeal in his behalf. This he did so eloquently, and built up hypotheses so rapidly, that some of the rougher element, afraid that his efforts might be effectual, became rather demonstrative, and crowded around him in a somewhat threatening manner. They were quieted, however, by a few positive words from old Tom. It was rather a decided but not particularly pleasant compliment to the youth's forensic ability !

When the defense had closed its wonderfully ingenious argument, the judge made another of his significant addresses in his charge to the jury, and a little after midnight he submitted the case to them.

An awful silence prevailed for a few moments while the twelve men put their heads together and consulted in a low tone without leaving their seats. Presently they all rose, and their spokesman, turning to the judge, uttered only one word: "GUILTY."

Then, at a sign from stern old Sam, who immediately came down from his pile of bacon, the two determined-faced miners, with Podgett between them almost paralyzed with fear, walked out into

"WITH PODGETT BETWEEN THEM."

the night, followed by the crowd, who fired off their pistols, and made the very hills tremble with their demoniacal yells.

The early morning sun, as its rays entered the narrow valley, shone upon the lifeless body of Podgett, where, suspended by the neck from the limb of a huge oak tree on the main street of Whooping Hollow, it slowly oscillated at the sport of the warm south breeze.

THE WOOING OF AH-KEY-NES-TOU.

MANDAN CHIEF.

A T a period late in the twenties, the Mandans, one of the most intelligent tribes of Indians on the continent, were almost swept out of existence by the small-pox. The story comes down to us in the form of a tradition among other savages, but it is nevertheless true, as there are a few old trappers yet living who remember all the particulars of the event.

The Mandans resided in the vicinity of the mouth of the Yellowstone, where their villages were permanent for untold centuries, and at the time of the visitation of the fell disease which nearly annihilated them they comprised about three thousand families.

Shortly after sunrise, one morning in June, 1828, a young white man was reclining idly on

one of the grassy knolls overlooking the village,
the great river, and the vast prairie stretching
westwardly from its bank. He was intently watching certain movements in the town, where the
warriors were preparing for a grand hunt. In
the distance, the buffalo could be seen grazing in
immense herds, whose presence was the cause of
the commotion among the Indians. Soon he saw
hundreds of warriors, armed with bows, their quiv-
ers filled with arrows, emerge from the shadow of
their lodges, and in a long line ride out toward
the unsuspecting animals so peacefully feeding.
The old men and squaws alone remained in the
village, and they were gathered in anxious groups,
applauding the husbands, sons and lovers as they
went proudly forth to battle for that subsistence
which was their only dependence when the snows
of winter filled the now sunny valley.

A few moments after the warriors had disappeared in the purple morning mist of the prairies,
a bevy of lightly dressed dusky maidens, in all
their savage beauty, wandered toward the sandy
margin of the Yellowstone to indulge in their
favorite amusement of swimming in its clear
sparkling tide,—for that stream in summer, like
a great brook, ripples and babbles over the
rounded quartz pebbles which compose its bed,

with as rhythmical a flow as the tiniest rivulet in the recesses of the mountains.

It was this group of Indian maidens that now attracted the gaze of the young stranger; one

among them particularly, not yet seventeen, but more beautiful than the others, walked like some society queen on the beach at Newport. In a few moments she purposely separated herself from the rest and directed her steps toward the mound

on which the young man was lying. He smiled
when he saw her evident intention, and a flush of
pride swept over his bronzed cheeks as he came
down to the base of the elevation to await her
approach.

The young girl thus seeking the intruder was
the affianced bride of "In-ne-cose" (The Iron
Horn), principal chief of the Mandans — old
enough to be her grandfather. She, the handsome Indian maiden, was known as "Ah-key-
nes-tou" (The Red Rose), and was the pride of
the Mandan nation.

The young man, who had with impatience
waited for her coming all the morning, was of
course an American; an incipient doctor who
had enlisted in the service of the great Fur Company a year before, whose agency was at the
junction of the Missouri and Yellowstone rivers,
near the Mandan village. He had imagined himself in love many times in St. Louis, where was
his home, but was now satisfied that he had
really never felt the tender passion until he saw
Ah-key-nes-tou at the general store one day, some
months before the story of their fate commences.

When he discovered that the beautiful girl was
destined to be the fifth wife of the old chief
In-ne-cose — a cross, ugly Indian, and moreover

not a full-blooded Mandan — he took pity on her, loved her more than ever, and resolved to win her for himself. Ah-key-nes-tou had often admitted to the "White Medicine," as the band of Mandans called the youthful doctor, that she had a decided predilection for him; that she could never love the old chief; but as her father had been paid for her by the present of two horses, she felt bound to the bargain according to Indian usage.

The doctor in a dozen interviews had told Ah-key-nes-tou of his deep love; that he was willing to leave his home forever for her sake, and, marrying her, would become an adopted son of the tribe. But poor "Ah-key," as her white admirer always called her, considered herself in honor bound to become the wife of In-ne-cose; consequently both the youth and the maiden were perfectly miserable.

In a few moments the doctor and Ah-key met at the foot of the mound, where, without speaking, they seated themselves on the grass with which the ground was covered. After looking at her silently for some time, he took the maiden's hand and said:

"It is a long time since Ah-key has come to her white lover. I have been very sad; the sun shone brightly, but I could not see its brightness, for you were far away. I learn that In-ne-cose intends soon to take you for his fifth wife. I want but one; you are that one; my lodge is empty — I cannot live without you."

The Indian maiden trembled for a moment, then answered: "Ah-key-nes-tou's heart is small, but it is very red. My father has given me to the great chief. Two lovers have come to me; my heart can hold but one. I see in it the face of my young White Medicine only; but a river as wide as the Missouri parts us. In-ne-cose has given two horses for me; my father has spoken; I must be the fifth wife of the great chief. What can I do ?"

The idea of Ah-key-nes-tou becoming the bride of any other than himself, made the young doctor almost wild, and he would have given vent to some very emphatic language had not the girl at that instant said to him: "There is a snake in the grass that the pale-face does not see," and she pointed with her tapering index-finger to a spot not far off, where' the weeds and sunflower-stalks seemed to move by some other power than the wind. It was In-ne-cose himself, who had stealthily followed and was watching Ah-key-nes-tou. "You must go to the village and eat with my people to-day," continued the trembling maiden, as she looked imploringly toward her lover.

The doctor was now satisfied they had a dangerous spy upon their actions, and grinding his teeth, hastened to obey her injunction at once. He dared not kiss Ah-key now, but they exchanged glances,—a language that is understood by all

MANDAN CANOE.

who love, whether white, black, or red; and as she walked away he shouldered his heavy rifle and ascended the knoll again, where he stood erect for a few minutes so that the whole village might see him. Remaining where he stood until Ah-key-nes-ton had rejoined the group of her friends on the beach, where they were preparing for their bath, the doctor descended, and moved quietly toward the nearest group of lodges.

First, he made a visit to that of a subordinate chief who was friendly to both Ah-key-nes-tou and himself, looking with decided favor on his efforts to win the girl. Then he went to the lodge of Ah-key-nes-tou's father. He was received very kindly, invited to breakfast, and when that was disposed of, the pipe was passed around, an evidence of the warm feeling the Indian entertained for his white guest. After some time devoted to the fragrant fumes of the "kin-ne-ke-nick," the doctor opened up the subject always nearest his heart—his desire to marry the old savage's daughter. The father of the girl freely admitted that he should be highly honored by such an alliance, but that his word had been pledged to the "Iron Horn," and as presents had been accepted from him, the matter must be considered as settled; that the tribe would never condone any deceit on his part—he could not break his word.

The doctor agreed with his honorable host, that the difficulties were great, according to the Indian code of honor; nevertheless, he believed that the thing could be so arranged that it would be acceptable to all concerned. He then informed the old man that a steamboat (or "fire-ship," as the

MANDAN VILLAGE.

savages called it,) would arrive at the village
that evening. On it were his trunk, tent, and all
his belongings; he proposed to take up his abode
with the tribe. To this, War Eagle, the father of
Ah-key-nes-tou, cordially gave his approval; sug-
gesting that the mound from which the villagers
had first seen him that morning would be a suitable place to establish his lodge.

Just before sunset the guns of the steamboat
were heard in the village as she rounded a sharp
point near her proposed landing-place. Immediately the entire population, men, women and
children, flocked to the beach to see the wonderful canoe that moved without oars. They regarded it as a monster, gazing upon it with fear
and trembling every time it came up the river.

Early the next morning, with the assistance of
some of his Mandan friends the doctor landed his
traps and erected his tent on the spot designated
by War Eagle. His equipments consisted of a
neat camp bed, rich blankets, arms, ammunition,
and a medicine chest, together with hundreds of
little trinkets pleasing to the taste of the Indians
of both sexes.

The enthusiastic young doctor had hardly gotten his things in shipshape before a messenger
from In-ne-cose arrived, demanding his presence

at the council lodge. He obeyed the summons from the head chief, of course, but he could not divine why he had been sent for so suddenly, just as he had fixed himself comfortably in his new home. Reaching the lodge where the chiefs and head men were assembled, he found there also many women and children of the tribe, evidently expectant of some serious matter to be discussed.

In-ne-cose sat in the center of his counselors, on a magnificently embroidered buffalo robe, smoking his great pipe trimmed with eagle-feathers, as stoical as an Egyptian mummy, excepting that around his mouth there played a smile of devilish import.

Standing near her father, who had also been summoned to the council, was Ah-key-nes-tou, dusky and beautiful in her savage grace, with a look of pride on her countenance; for was it not certain that she was to be the subject for discussion by the suddenly assembled warriors?

Wrapped around the shoulders of the stern In-ne-cose was a curiously wrought Mexican blanket, the sight of which, as the doctor's eyes fell upon it, caused his whole frame to tremble. He turned pale, and his entire aspect was that of fear and deep solicitude; but not a word did he utter.

As soon as those who were called to the council had seated themselves, In-ne-cose rose and said:

"A pale-faced medicine-man has fixed his lodge by those of the Mandans. We have plenty of ground here.; there are great herds of buffalo roaming over the prairie, which the Great Spirit has sent to furnish food for his people; the rich young warrior with a white skin is welcome to his share of these. His heart is red, and he is the friend of the Mandans. But he is alone; he has no squaw to cook his meat or saddle his horse; no one to make his bed of the soft skins of the buffalo; no one to shape the moccasins for his feet; he has no wife to bring home the game that he kills. He cannot get a slave to do all these things, for we are at peace with every nation; there is no war. He must therefore take a wife from among the young women of the Mandans; there are many. He can buy two wives, for he is rich; let him choose when In-ne-cose takes Ah-key-nes-tou. I have said."

The doctor immediately arose from his place, full of indignation and disgust at the old chief's cunning. Familiar with the language of the tribe, he addressed the assembled warriors in their own tongue. All eyes were riveted on him, for the majority of those present, and many who were absent, were in perfect accord with him in his honorable efforts to win Ah-key-nes-tou from the "Iron Horn," whom they feared but did not respect.

"In-ne-cose is a dog!" boldly began the doctor. The chiefs gazed upon him with wonderment, but without betraying any emotion. "The Great Spirit is angry," continued the orator. "In-ne-cose is a vulture among eagles, and would carry off the prettiest eaglet. But the Great Spirit says that it shall not be so. Before the sun goes down seven times more, In-ne-cose will be dead! He will take with him to the happy hunting-grounds many Mandan warriors; many young women and children — perhaps Ah-key-nes-tou;" and the young man was deeply affected. He merely added the chief's own words, "I have said," then sat down.

In a few moments, when his feelings had partially regained their normal state, he rose again to explain to the now bewildered and wondering warriors and women what he meant by the awful prophecy he had just uttered. He told them that on the passage of the steamboat up the river, only two days before she had landed at their village, a Mexican merchant on board had died of a frightful disease, the smallpox! He explained how ter-

ribly contagious it was to those who were not
guarded against it by a great medicine operation
performed by the white man. That the merchant
who had died of the disease possessed a blanket,
upon which he had breathed his last. In-ne-cose
had stolen that blanket off the boat, and had it
now wrapped around him. He told them that
every Indian who went near him, who touched
that blanket, or even breathed the same air
where he sat, would die unless with his medicine
he could save them. The doctor continued:

"The Great Spirit is very angry. Darkness is
coming over the lodges of the Mandans. In less
than one moon, perhaps, not a lodge will be full.
You love Ah-key-nes-tou; let her go to the lodge
of the pale-faced Medicine Man, and he will go to
that of the 'Iron Horn'—but I fear it is too late."

By the time the doctor had completed his remarks so fraught with portent, all those assembled within the council lodge rapidly moved
themselves from the presence of In-ne-cose. He
however sat stoically smoking, apparently not
the least disturbed by the fearful predictions of
the doctor. In a few moments the old chief rose
again, and thus addressed himself to the pre-
sumptuous white man:

"The Great Spirit lives in the clouds. If he

wills that all my people shall go to him, they must obey. My little ones slept on the mystery blanket last night; they awoke this morning and were well. Will the Bad Spirit touch them?"

Then drawing the "death-blanket" closer around him, In-ne-cose apparently defied the evil effects of the wrap. But shortly afterward his dusky skin showed a slight pallor and he seemed strangely agitated. He again spoke, though this time in a disturbed voice, addressing himself, as before, directly to the doctor:

"The chief of the Mandans is rich. He has four squaws already. If the young pale-face will drive away the Bad Spirit from the little ones of In-ne-cose, he may take Ah-key-nes-tou for his wife."

The doctor, delighted at these words of the head chief, grasped the old man's hand, and told him that he would do his best to save the children. Then, ordering Ah-key-nes-tou's brother to lead his sister to his lodge on the knoll, he told another Indian to go and bring his medicine chest to the lodge of In-ne-cose. He then went to the chief's lodge himself, but on examining the little ones discovered it was too late for vaccination: the blanket had done its work !

The next day the pestilence broke out in a hun-

dred lodges. Very soon the Indians were not able
to bury their dead — the latter outnumbering the
living. In less than a month, out of three thou-'
sand families only eight survived. Where the
Mandan village once stood, even as late as thirty
years ago the traces of over eight thousand graves
could be seen. It was an awful visitation, almost
annihilating a whole nation !

In-ne-cose, as predicted by the doctor, was the
first to die. Ah-key-nes-tou was saved by prompt
vaccination. The doctor took her to St. Louis,
where they were married, the ceremony being
performed by that grand and good old Catholic
priest, Father DeSmet, who was stationed there
at the time, and whose memory is kept green by
every tribe of Indians on the continent. Ah-key-
nes-tou was educated at one of the convents in
the Mound City, became the pet of society, and
her worthy husband a State Senator.

KIT CARSON.

I HAVE been requested by several parties to offer something of Kit Carson's early days on the Plains. Having been intimate with that famous man during the declining years of his eventful life, and having heard from his own lips many of the adventures of his youth, while sitting around the camp-fire on several little "outings" with him and Maxwell in the mountains of New Mexico, I have chosen for my sketch Kit's first shot at an Indian.

That portion of the great central plains of Kansas which radiates from the Pawnee Fork as its center, including the bend of the Arkansas, where that river makes a sudden sweep to the

southeast, and the beautiful valley of the Walnut,—in all an area of nearly a thousand square
miles,—was from time immemorial a sort of de-
batable ground, occupied by none of the tribes,
but claimed by all to hunt in, for it was a famous
resort of the buffalo.

None of the various bands of savages had the
temerity to attempt its permanent occupancy, for
whenever they met there—which was of frequent
occurrence—on their annual hunt for their winter's supply of meat, a bloody battle was sure to
ensue. The region referred to has perhaps been
the scene of more sanguinary conflicts than any
other portion of the continent. Particularly was
this the case when the Pawnees, who claimed the
country, met their hereditary enemies, the Cheyennes.

Through this region, hugging the margin of
the silent Arkansas, and running under the very
shadow of Pawnee Rock, the old Santa Fé trail
wound its course, now the actual road-bed of the
Santa Fe Railway,—so closely are the past and
present transcontinental highways cemented at
this point: one, a mere memory; the other, one
of the great railways now spanning the continent.

Who, among the bearded and grizzled old fel-
lows like myself, has forgotten that most exciting
—17

and sensational (at least it was so to my boyish
mind) of all the miserably executed illustrations
in the geographies of their school-days fifty years
ago—"Santa Fé Traders Attacked by Indians" ?
The picture located the scene of the fight at Pawnee Rock, which formed a sort of a nondescript
shadow in the background of a crudely drawn
representation of the dangers of the trail.

I witnessed a spirited encounter between a small
band of the Cheyennes and Pawnees in the fall of
1867.   It occurred on the open prairie, just north
of the mouth of the Walnut, about four miles
from where the city of Great Bend now stands.
Both tribes were hunting the buffalo, and when
each by accident discovered the presence of the
other, with a demoniacal yell that fairly shook
the sand-dunes of the Arkansas they rushed at
once into the shock of battle.

The Pawnees were of course friendly to the
whites, and had permission from their agent to
leave their reservation in the valley of the Neosho, near Council Grove.   At that particular
time, for a wonder, the Cheyennes too were temporarily at peace with the Government.   So I had
nothing to do but passively witness the savage
combat.

Both bands of the savages soon exhausted their

ammunition, and then the chiefs of the contending factions appealed to me most earnestly to supply them with more, of which there was plenty at Fort Zarah, only half a mile away. I was necessarily forced to remain neutral, but my sympathies were with the "under dog" in the fight, —which happened to be the Cheyennes, whom the Pawnees drove off disgraced and discomfitted.

That evening, in a grove of timber on the Walnut, the victors had a grand dance in which scalps, ears and fingers of their enemy, suspended by strings to poles, were important accessories to their weird orgies around the huge camp-fires.

How true it is, as Longfellow declares: "The thoughts of youth are long, long thoughts." I remember that map in the geographies of fifty years ago (already referred to) on which was depicted "the Great American Desert," over which I pored in the little log school-house at the cross-roads in the country, near my home in one of the Eastern States. How distinctly I remember seeing Bent's old fort marked on the western edge of the "Desert" on that quaint map. Then, in the "long, long thoughts" of my boyhood's fancy, it seemed to me to be away out on the confines of another world, for then I had never been thirty miles away from the farm on which I was reared.

I have slept under the old fort's hospitable roof many times since, but long before the era of railroads, where, gathered around its huge adobe fireplaces, up whose cavernous throats the yellow flames crackled and roared, were the mighty men of the Ute nation, with Kit Carson, Lucien B. Maxwell, Bent, and other famous characters of the border, conversing in the beautiful but silent sign-language, that is so perfect in its symbolization. Of those who were present then, all but myself are long since dead, and the scenes of those days are only hidden pictures in the storehouse of my brain, to be called back in the quiet of the gloaming, with their host of accompanying pleasant memories of a shadowy past.

In my boyhood days I honestly believed that Kit Carson was at least eight feet tall; that he always dressed in the traditional buckskin, fringed at the seams, and beaded and "porcupined" all over; that he carried innumerable eleven-inch bowie-knives, his rifle of huge dimensions — so large and heavy that, like Warwick's sword, no ordinary man could even lift it. I believed his regular meal to be an entire buffalo, which he raised with both hands to his mouth, and picked its immense bones as easily as the average mortal does a chicken's wing, and that he drank out of nothing smaller than a river. Boys, probably by the thousands, had the same "long thoughts," for boy-nature is the same everywhere.

Kit Carson was really a man under the average height, rather delicate-looking in physical make-up than otherwise, but in fact, wiry and quick, though cautious, possessing nerves of steel and an imperturbability in the moment of supreme danger that was marvelous to contemplate.

He was fond of cards and horse-racing, a famous rider in his younger days, having entered the lists in many a contest with the Indians, who are generally passionately devoted to trials of speed between rival ponies. I have myself seen, in the long-ago, as many as eight hundred horses bet by contending bands, whose wealth was counted by the number of animals they possessed.

Kit once, years before he became famous, fought a duel, mounted; he escaped with a bullet-wound behind his left ear, the scar of which he carried to his grave, but he winged his equally youthful antagonist in the quarrel.

Kit's nature was composed of the noblest of attributes: he was brave, but never reckless like Custer; unselfish, a veritable exponent of Christian altruism; and as true to his friends as steel to the magnet.

He died in 1868, at Fort Lyon, on the Arkansas, while on his way to Fort Harker to make me a long - promised visit. For some time after his passing away he rested peacefully under the gnarled and knotted old cottonwoods which fringe the river—that Nile of America—in the vicinity of Lyon. Later, his remains were moved to Taos, his former New Mexico home, where an appropriate monument was erected over them; in the plaza of quaint and curious Santa Fé, too, there is a massive cenotaph which records his deeds and name.

Kit was born in Kentucky, on the 24th of December, 1809. While a mere infant his parents emigrated to what is now Howard county, Missouri, which at that early date was literally a "howling wilderness" filled with "varmints" of all kinds.

There, as soon as he was big enough to lift a rifle, the old-fashioned patch-and-ball, flint-lock affair, the embryo great frontiersman began to hunt, and by the time he was fifteen he became the most expert shot in the whole settlement. He could hit the eye of a squirrel every time he pulled the trigger, or it didn't count.

At this period, however, his father apprenticed him to a saddler, with whom he worked faithfully

for two years, spending all his leisure moments
in the primitive forest, hunting bear, deer, and
other large game that abounded there.

In two years more, when Kit had reached the age
of seventeen, the trade with Santa Fé began, with
its initial point in the hamlet of Old Franklin, in
Howard county, near where Kit lived (from which
place it did not move to Independence until 1886).

In the late spring of 1826, Col. St. Vrain, a
prominent agent of the great fur companies, (a
grand old gentleman whom I knew intimately,)
arrived at Franklin and made preparations to fit
out a large caravan destined for the far-off Rocky
Mountains, loaded with goods to be used in trad-
ing with the Indians for the skins of the valuable
fur-bearing animals of that remote and but little
known region.

Kit, as green as any boy of his age who had
never been twenty miles from his home, was in-
fatuated by the stories told by the old trappers of
the Colonel's outfit, regarding the wonderful game
in the land to which they were going, and he was
easily persuaded to join the caravan in the capacity of hunter, his prowess with the rifle having
reached the ears of the major-domo of the train.
Kit ran away from home, I suspect, though he
never told me so.

The expedition was composed of twenty-six mule-wagons, some loose stock, and forty-two men. In addition to his employment as hunter, young Kit was to help drive the extra animals, take his turn in standing guard, and make himself generally useful.

The party marched wearily along, day after day, Kit proving his right to the reputation of being a mighty hunter, without any adventure worthy of recording, until they arrived at the Walnut, where they discovered the first signs of Indians. They had halted for that day; the mules were unharnessed, the camp-fires lighted, and the men about to indulge in their ever-welcome black coffee, when they were suddenly surprised by half a dozen Pawnees, who, mounted on their ponies, hideously painted and uttering the most diabolical yells, rushed out of the tall grass on the Arkansas bottom, and swinging their buffalo robes attempted to stampede the animals of the caravan.

Every man in the outfit was on his feet in an instant with his rifle in hand, so that all the impudent savages got for their pains were a few harmless shots as they scampered back to the river and over into the sand-hills out of sight.

The next night the caravan camped at the foot

of Pawnee Rock, and of course, after the experience of the afternoon before, every precaution was employed to prevent another surprise. The wagons were formed into a corral, so that the animals might be protected in the event of a prolonged fight with the savages. The guards were instructed to be doubly vigilant, and every man slept with his rifle on his arm, for the old Colonel assured them the savages would never rest content with their defeat on the Walnut, but true to their thieving propensities and their desire for revenge, would seize the first favorable opportunity to renew the attack.

All this was a new and strange experience to young Carson, who had never before seen any Indians except a few friendly Shawnees and Osages. Of the methods and tactics of the wild Plains tribes, he literally knew nothing.

When everything was arranged for the night, Kit was posted as a sentinel immediately in front of the south face of the Rock, nearly two hundred yards from the wagon corral. The other men who were on guard were posted on top, and on the open prairie on either side.

About half-past eleven, as near as he could guess, Kit told me, one of the guards yelled out "Indians!" and ran the mules that were grazing near, into the corral, while the entire company turned out of their blankets on the report of a rifle on the midnight air coming from the direction of the Rock.

In a few minutes young Kit came running down toward the corral, where the men had collected, and Col. St. Vrain asked him if he had seen any Indians.

THE TRAIN AT PAWNEE ROCK.

"Yes," replied Kit, "I killed one of the red devils — I saw him fall."

There was no further disturbance that night; it proved to be a false alarm; so all who were not standing guard that night were soon peacefully sleeping again.

The next morning at the first streak of day, every one was up and anxious to see young Carson's dead Indian. They went out *en masse* to the Rock, when instead of finding a painted Pawnee, they discovered Kit's riding-mule, dead — shot through the head.

The boy felt terribly mortified over his ridiculous blunder, and it was a long time before he heard the last of his midnight shot at his mule.

He explained to me the circumstances: He had not slept any the previous night, and he had watched so earnestly for a chance to kill a Pawnee that he supposed he must have fallen asleep leaning against the face of the Rock; "but I was wide enough awake to hear the cry of 'Indians!'" said he. "I had picketed my mule about twenty steps from where I stood, and I suppose it had been lying down. All I know is that the first thing I saw after the alarm was something rising up out of the grass. I thought sure it was an Indian; I took aim, and pulled the trigger. It was a center shot; I don't believe that mule kicked once after he was hit!"

In the morning, a few minutes after the men had returned from a visit to Kit's dead mule, a real battle commenced. The Pawnees attacked the camp in earnest, and kept the little outfit busy all that day, the next night, and till the following night—nearly three whole days, the animals all that time shut up in the corral without food or water.

On the second midnight the men harnessed up and attempted to drive out, but were driven back and had to give it up.

The third night, just before morning, they tried it again, determined to reach the ford at Pawnee Rock to water their animals, or all would perish. It was a little more than ten miles distant from the Rock (and is now within the corporate limits of Larned).

They succeeded in keeping off the savages, and arrived at the ford in comparative safety. The trail at that point crossed the creek in the shape of a horseshoe; or rather, in consequence of a double bend in the stream as it debouches into the Arkansas, the road crossed it twice, as all who have traveled the old Santa Fé trail in the early days will remember.

In making this crooked passage many of the wagons were badly wrecked in the creek, because the mules were terribly thirsty, and their drivers could not control them.

The caravan was hardly "strung out" again on the opposite bank of the Pawnee, when the Indians poured a shower of arrows and a volley of bullets from both sides of the trail into the train. But before they could reload or draw their arrows a desperate charge was made among them, headed by the Colonel, and it took only a few minutes to clear out the savages, and then the caravan moved on.

During the whole fight at the Rock and at Pawnee Fork, the party lost four men killed, seven wounded, and eleven mules killed (not including Kit's), and twenty wounded.

From this fight Kit said Pawnee Rock was named.

A THEORY AS TO GEN. CUSTER'S DEATH.

GEN. GEORGE A. CUSTER.

LITTLE is known of the origin of scalp-taking, and that, vague and indefinite: nearly every tribe has some wild, weird legend to account for the custom, but these traditions vary widely as to·the cause. That "raising the hair" of an enemy is of great antiquity, there is no doubt, as in the Bible it is related how the soldiers tore the skin from the heads of their whipped foes. All, or at least all Indian tribes with which I am acquainted, scalp their enemies killed in battle.

With the Indian there appears to be some close affiliation between the departed spirit and his hair. I have questioned many a blood-begrimed warrior why he should want a dead man's hair,

and invariably there have been assigned a number
of reasons, three of which are most prominent:
First, it is an evidence to his people that he has
triumphed over an enemy; second, the scalps are
employed very prominently in the incantations of
the "medicine lodge"—a part of their religious
rites; third, the savage believes there is a wonderfully inherent power in the scalp of an enemy.
All the excellent qualities of the victim go with
his hair the moment it is wrenched from his head.
If it be that of a renowned warrior, so much the
more are they anxious to procure his scalp, for
the fortunate possessor then inherits all the
bravery and prowess of its original owner.

I have known of but one instance in all my experience among the Indians, where a white man
taken prisoner in battle escaped death. It was a
great many years ago; the party, a dear friend,
still living, was a grand old mountaineer,—but
the homeliest man on earth, probably. He was
red-faced, wrinkled, and pockmarked, with a
mouth as large and full of teeth as a gorilla's,
and there was no more hair on any part of his
head than there is on the head of a cane. He
was captured in a prolonged fight and taken to
the village of the tribe where the principal chief
resided. The latter gave one look at the prisoner,

shook his head, and said he was "bad medicine ";
that if he was not the "evil spirit" himself, he
was closely allied to him. He then ordered his
subordinates to furnish him with a pony, loaded
him with provisions, provided him with a rifle,
and told him to go to his people. This incident,
which is a fact, shows that you cannot account
for the occasional vagaries of the North-American
savage.

The Indians of the Plains and Rocky Mountains
would rather, for the reason last above stated,
take one scalp of a famous scout or army officer
who has successfully chastised them, like Custer,
Sully, and Crook, than a dozen of those of ordinary white men.

Twenty-six years ago next November I was
camping on the high "divide" between the
Arkansas river and the Beaver, with a party
of Government Indian scouts, members of three
friendly tribes,— Osages, Pawnees, and Kaws,—
employed by order of Gen. Sheridan in his winter
campaign against the hostile Cheyennes, Arapahoes, and Kiowas. It was a terribly gusty day,
one of those so characteristic of our Plains region
at certain times of the year. As with closely
wrapped blankets we huddled around our little
fire of buffalo-chips, the dust and ashes would

rise in miniature whirlwinds and go dancing over the prairies until they exhausted themselves.

I asked a venerable chief of the Osages who was present, "Little River," nearly eighty years old, what those fitful spirals indicated, in order to draw from his savage mind his ideas of the forces of nature. He replied: "They are the spirits of some southern Indians, killed and scalped up north, going back to the lodges of their people."

I thought that if he had substituted the word "matter" for "spirit"—for every-

LITTLE RIVER.

where we tread upon the dust of a lost civilization — probably he would have been nearer the truth than in the statement of one of the superstitions of his race.

Among the many myths of the American savage, the disposition of the soul after its separation from the body, and its close connection with its scalp, vary according to the religion of the tribe. With some, the "journey to the happy hunting-
—18

grounds" begins immediately; with others, the spirit remains near the grave. Again, if an Indian dies away from the lodges of his people, the spirit returns at once to them, where it hovers, as if reluctant to leave. Among the "upper-river tribes" it is believed that before the spirit finally departs from those who have died of wounds received in battle, "it floats toward a great cliff overhanging the Missouri, and carves upon the wall of rock a picture showing the manner of death." It is believed by most Plains tribes that the soul attaches itself to the scalp; that the soul of a person scalped does not suffer from the wounds inflicted on the body, but that the converse is the case where the scalp is not torn off.

There are many instances on record where men have been scalped and yet survived the terrible ordeal, but in every case the scalper supposed his victim dead, the latter taking good care that the foeman should not be disabused of the supposed fact.

One who kills himself in battle, accidentally or purposely, has positively no hereafter; he is irrevocably lost. Those who are struck by lightning, or die by any other apparently direct operation of the "Manitou" (the Great Spirit), are hurriedly buried where they fall, without any ceremony, and no mound or other mark is erected over them. If after a battle there are found corpses not scalped or their bodies not mutilated, it is certain that those persons came to death by their own hand, for it is part of the religion of an Indian not to scalp or mutilate the body of an enemy who commits suicide. His superstition in regard to persons dying by suicide or by lightning is as religiously observed as any other of his myths.

Knowing this deep-rooted superstition as well as I do, I have been led to believe — though the statement may provoke discussion among those who know nothing of the Indian character — that the death of the lamented Gen. Custer in that awfully unequal battle of the "Little Big Horn" was not according to the accepted theory at that time, viz. : that he was killed by the Indian chief "Rain-in-the-face." The tale (which I regard as an idle fiction so far as the facts are concerned) as it has been told a thousand times and copied in the newspapers of the world, is, that one day the General's brother Tom, at one of the military posts where the regiment to which he was attached, the famous Seventh Cavalry (commanded by the General), was stationed, had a dispute with Rain-in-the-face, and struck him. The savage was furious with rage, but suppressed it, and mounting his pony rode off sullenly to his lodge.

Years after the death of Gen. Custer, Rain-in-the-face, who unquestionably participated in the battle of the Rosebud (as the action is sometimes called), is said to have related that he killed Gen. Custer, thus avenging himself for the indignity put upon himself by the General's brother Tom, so long before. In all probability the story was made out of "whole cloth" by a certain New York newspaper correspondent, in whose journal it first appeared. I knew him well, and his reputation for unexaggerated truth was far from being as orthodox as he of the cherry-tree fame. Because it had a plausibility about it, and was highly sensational, the statement was accepted by the general public, or those who were not familiar with the methods of the North-American savage. No doubt Rain-in-the-face did, as would all Indians, treasure up such a grievance as that of having been insulted by a blow from a white man; but the circumstances of the battle of the Little Big Horn in all its horrors, so far as it is possible to know them, preclude the possibility of Sitting Bull permitting a subordinate chief, as was Rain-in-the-face, to arrogate to himself the right of revenge in the case of such a noted "white warrior" as Custer. If by any probability Rain-in-the-face did kill Custer, he certainly would have scalped him and mutilated his body. Custer was

not scalped, nor was his person at all abused; and the reason generally given for this immunity from the common custom of savage warfare is, that the Indians had such a profound admiration for his wonderful bravery that they spared the great "white warrior" that humiliation. This is the weakest point of the whole argument—for the greater the man in the savages' estimation, the more eager would they be to secure his scalp.

My own theory is—and the fact that Custer was not scalped or mutilated is not the only confirmation of it—that the General killed himself to escape the horrible torture that awaited him should he be captured alive. His capture was what Sitting Bull had undoubtedly determined upon, the moment he saw the tide of battle unmistakably turning in his favor.

Custer was known to all the Plains tribes; he had given them ample cause to remember him, and these savages would never have allowed an opportunity to capture him alive to be defeated by permitting some aggrieved chief to kill him in order to gratify a personal revenge—the game was too big. The Indians called Custer the "Crawling Panther," because he usually fell upon them with his troopers as stealthily as does that animal upon its prey.

To those unacquainted with the methods of the American savage of the Great Plains, the statement that suicide would be infinitely preferable to the chances for life after having been captured by the Indians, may seem overdrawn, and wicked to be thought of. But if they had seen, as I have, the remains of men, women and innocent babes horribly mutilated, burnt, butchered, and hacked to pieces, they too, if they knew such a fate awaited them beyond the possibility of a doubt if captured alive, would unhesitatingly court death by their own hands, suddenly and immediately, rather than wait for the other, a few hours or days more remote, perhaps, but certain, and horrible in its prolonged agony.

I know that it was commonly understood, if not actually agreed to among the officers at frontier posts, that each one should reserve the last bullet in his revolver for himself in the event of a horrible contingency. I have known of many officers in the long-ago of my early service among the Indians, who, whenever they went on an expedition against the hostile tribes, invariably had concealed about their persons, easily accessible, a small capsule of prussic acid or some equally potent and swift messenger of death, to be used in case of a possible contingency.

Custer, it will be remembered, was shot through the head, and it was a curious coincidence that two or three of his subordinates whose bodies were found near his had been shot in precisely the same manner.

In view of all these facts, there can be small doubt that those officers carried out the plan of death determined upon, the moment they recognized the hopelessness of their situation.

That the story of Rain-in-the-face, if he ever told it, is not at all likely to be the truth, may be inferred from the fact that the average Indian, as I know him, when discoursing of his own prowess is the most unconscionable liar, and the truth is not in him. Of course if Rain-in-the-face could prevail upon a newspaper correspondent to flatter him in regard to the part he took in a battle in which a great white warrior was defeated, he would rather lie to that correspondent than not; and that is just what Rain-in-the-face did in this instance — provided, always, that the correspondent did not invent the whole tale.

The truth of how Custer came to his death can never absolutely be known, for out of that awfully unequal conflict there came but one miserable Crow Indian and Col. Keogh's celebrated horse "Comanche," alive. From the fact that the great soldier was not scalped, the theory I have suggested is certainly more plausible, and will be accepted by all who are familiar with the customs of the Indians, than that story which has made the rounds of the newspapers a dozen times.